CRUEL LUST

ELITE MAFIA OF NEW YORK SERIES

MISSY WALKER

Cover Design: Missy Walker

Editor: Swish Design & Editing

To Mr Walker. This would be possible without you, but having you by my side makes it so much more fun and a helluva lot easier x

1

EMILIA

This is it.

When they look back over the course of my stellar career as one of the youngest people to ever make detective in the entire state of New York, this is where the story will begin.

The night I first made contact with the Santoro family before I eventually took them down.

"Explain something to me," my partner pushes, slamming his door after stepping out of the car and staring at me over the roof. "What do you think we're going to find here tonight?"

If I grit my teeth any harder, they're going to crack. I am so sick of his misogynistic bullshit, not to mention the way he talks down to me. As if his ten years as a detective somehow earns him the right to treat me like a child.

He's no different than any other stupid, egotistical man I've ever dealt with. Unfortunately, I'm forced to spend time with him. But you can't choose your partner.

I'm sure it was supposed to ease me into my role as a

detective, pairing me with a ten-year veteran such as Craig Graham when I joined the unit six months ago. However, I would probably do better on my own since all he does is hold me back and ask stupid, pointless questions that only serve to waste time.

The way he is right now as we stand in a parking lot across the street from one of the city's hottest clubs, it wouldn't surprise me if he only agreed to this little field trip to watch me fail and take me down a peg.

And I get it, in a way. I don't expect anyone from the Santoro family to commit a punishable offense in front of us. They are the *Famiglia*, after all, one of the most ruthless mafia in New York. And if I take them down, then maybe the unit will treat me like I'm not just a useless rookie. But the Santoros won't slip up. They're much more discreet than that, considering the DA has been fighting to put together a case that sticks for years. Until now, the family has been a living, breathing piece of Teflon.

Everything beads up and rolls straight off them.

It infuriates me.

That's why I wanted in on this case and nagged my captain for the last month and dragged my partner here tonight. I have this burning need to show myself that justice can win in the end, and I truly believe I'm the one who can make it happen.

I can't throw Craig's words back in his face and tell him exactly what I think of his outdated and downright sexist opinions. My only hope for justice is to finally build a case against the Santoros and their biggest rivals, the Vitalis. The two families who have torn the city apart and gotten more than one innocent bystander caught up in their decades-old feud.

Tonight is the first step—if I can convince this caveman we're doing the right thing.

"How are we ever going to nail these guys unless we get a better idea of how they think? How they do business? If we're going to do what nobody's been able to do before, we need to take a different approach," I mutter as we make our way across the street.

As soon as he smirks, looking me up and down, I know what the jerk is thinking and have to stifle the sigh threatening to escape. "You're off to a good start. Where have you been hiding that body?"

His words make my skin crawl, but sadly, it's typical. "If I didn't know better, I would think you're making a case to be put on administrative leave." I come to a stop on the sidewalk, folding my arms. "But that can't possibly be what you have in mind, can it? Making sexist comments like that?" I question, raising an eyebrow.

He rolls his eyes before scoffing loudly. "Take it easy, would you? This isn't a *Me Too* story. But don't pretend you didn't put on that dress and those shoes to——"

"I'm trying to blend in," I inform him, cutting him off and gritting my teeth again at his bullshit to avoid an attention-grabbing fight on the sidewalk. "What, you think I'm going to walk in there with my badge on a lanyard around my neck? Get real."

He hoots with laughter behind me when I turn on my heel and march to the back of a long but quick-moving line separated from pedestrians by a velvet rope.

"You know I like it when you get sassy, Emilia," he remarks, and I can only roll my eyes before shivering a little when a stiff breeze blows past, knowing that no matter what I say, it will never be enough.

Shaking my head, I wrap my arms around myself to fight off the bite in the air. It's kind of chilly, and I am wearing less clothing than I'm used to. My idea of a comfortable outfit involves jeans and a sweater. Not four-inch stilettos and a dress that only reaches my mid-thigh while exposing more cleavage than I think I've ever revealed in public.

At least I know I blend in like I intended. A cluster of girls in front of us are dressed the same as me, and the mixed perfumes, hairspray, and lotion are almost enough to give me a headache.

"Here's one thing you need to keep in mind." Craig bends a little to speak

directly into my ear. "Try not looking like you're going to a funeral. You're

supposed to be having fun, right?"

There go my teeth, gritting again. This time, it's because he has a point. I deliberately relax my jaw and roll my shoulders back so I don't look quite so defensive. Sweeping my long, chestnut hair over one shoulder, I bat my eyelashes and pout my lips. "Is that better?" I ask in a breathy voice.

His eyes harden before he smirks. "Careful, Washington. You might end up signing a check you can't cash." After giving my cleavage a pointed, prolonged look, he stands straight and ushers me forward when the line moves again.

Men. It takes literally nothing to distract them. But I'm not going to be distracted tonight. I need my eyes open and my head clear. Until now, I've only set my sights on the Santoro family through news reports, photos in the paper, and the extensive intel gathered at the depot. The *capo*, Rocco Santoro, would never show his face in a place like this.

For one thing, he's too old-school and well past his partying days. My research into the family has given me a decent idea of what he likes to do for fun— theater, restaurants, and concerts. The rumors say he's gotten into gardening in his old age. Less murder, more mulching.

On the other hand, his two sons have been known to frequent one of the family's few legit businesses. Dante is the eldest and the family underboss. He wouldn't run this kind of establishment, not when he's overseeing so many of the family's other interests.

It's Luca, the second son, who prizes this club so highly.

And it's Luca I'm hoping to set eyes on tonight.

Once we make it to the front of the line and pay our cover charge, I remove my driver's license from my wallet, figuring somebody who looks as young as I do would get carded, and the last thing I need is someone seeing my badge.

As I breeze past the bouncer without so much as a second look, I am swiftly welcomed inside, and a nagging thought arises. *Are the long hours I've put into my work starting to show on my young face?*

Taking a deep breath, I push forward. At first, the darkness surrounding us is disorienting, but once we're past the coat check, the narrow hall opens into an enormous club. Flashing white, blue, and purple lights illuminate a long bar set against the wall to my left, spanning the room from front to back and already six customers deep.

Along the back wall and to my right are dimly lit and discreet booths. The sunken dance floor is already full of writhing bodies driven by an upbeat song pounding through speakers throughout the space. The floor's vibrations travel up through my body until it feels like I'm part of the room itself.

"Come on. Let's get a drink, at least." Craig scoffs at our surroundings like he's unimpressed before he leads the way, and for the first time tonight, I'm actually glad he's with me. Although highly fucking annoying, his larger body parts the crowd easily, and I follow on his heels like a running back taking advantage of the blocker in front of them.

A running back in needle-thin stilettos.

One thing is for sure. This place is much more upscale than I imagined. It's not some hole-in-the-wall dive where thugs gather to conduct their shady business.

I run a hand over the smooth marble bar after Craig elbows his way through. "White wine," I shout to Craig, who places the order with a handsome bartender while I scan the room.

There's a roped-off section in the back corner, and I instantly recognize a few faces at a semi-circular booth from countless award shows and movies. I guess it doesn't matter that a crime family runs this club.

Maybe they don't know...

... or maybe they do, and they don't care.

Either way, it's none of my business.

What is my business, though, is the young man in a dark suit who approaches the table and shakes hands with everyone seated there. He waves over a pretty girl wearing a black dress shorter than mine, who presents a bottle of champagne.

Luca Santoro.

Goose bumps cover my arms, and my heart skips a beat. He's gorgeous, but then I knew that, with jet black hair and a jaw sharp enough to cut glass. But there are some things a photo on a website can't convey. Like the way his smile seems to brighten everything around him. His easy laugh—I can't hear him from here, but I see the way everyone around him reacts. He's good at handling people. It's obvious this is the right sort of business for him to run.

When he leans down and murmurs something in the ear of that actress from the new Marvel movie, she blushes under the light hanging above the table and swats playfully at his arm. Something about their casual flirtation leaves a sour taste in my mouth.

Thanks, I mouth to Craig once he hands me a glass. "Be right back."

"What are you doing?" he questions, his deep voice ringing out over the chatter surrounding us, but I ignore it in favor of the instincts pushing me forward.

The wild thumping of the music is nothing compared to the pounding of my heart as I elbow my way through groups of people, always keeping one eye on Luca. I don't want him to get away. I can't let him slip away. Bringing him down means so much more than just catching a culprit. It's about finally getting the recognition I've worked tirelessly for all these years. Those countless nights spent working instead of going out with friends or dating someone.

Nowadays, my friends rarely invite me to hang out, and the few boyfriends I had couldn't handle how committed I was to my job. But despite all that, I'm still holding onto the hope that the sacrifices I've made might be worth it if I can succeed now.

Is this crazy?

Maybe.

But it could be my only shot of getting close to him. And for some reason, that seems more important than anything else.

Desperation floods my veins when he turns away from the table, and I move faster, turning the corner. Now, we're approaching each other, two speeding cars on a collision course. And once he's close enough, I make a point to stumble and spill my wine before falling against him.

Right away, the mountain-size man hovering behind him gets between us and takes my shoulders in his massive hands. "I'm sorry!" I gasp, swaying unsteadily. "I'm so sorry! Did I get you?"

Luca sizes me up in a single glance, then gives his bodyguard a look. Like magic, the man's hands are off my shoulders, and Luca steps closer. "I'm sorry. I must not have been looking where I was going."

He's not what I expected. I figured he would be annoyed and short-tempered. I definitely splashed his jacket. But all I see in his dark eyes is warmth and concern. Well, he is a businessman. I doubt he'd get far if word spread of him screaming at one of his customers for something so trivial.

My heels still put me at a disadvantage against his towering height. He has to bend to speak close to my ear. "Or maybe I was blinded by you. I've never seen you around here before." From this vantage point, I catch a glimpse of ink peeking out from beneath the top two popped buttons of his shirt. It looks like the top of an N and a T. *Santoro?*

Does he have his family name tattooed on his chest?

A sick chill runs down my spine when his breath fans across my ear and my neck. This is a murderer. At the very least, he turns a blind eye to what his family does. Either way, he's detestable and disgusting.

What a shame he smells so good. Spicy and musky combined with his charming grin leaves me reminding myself of who I'm dealing with. "I really am sorry. I'm so clumsy. And it is kind of dark in here." I bite my lip and twirl a strand of hair around my finger because why not? Why not sell the innocent act?

His grin widens into a smile that reminds me of a shark. "It's easier to do bad things in the dark, isn't it?" he remarks in a low tone. An involuntary shiver runs up my spine, and it takes everything I have to ignore it.

I already knew he was dangerous.

But when a flush heats my body and makes me lose my breath, it occurs to me I had no idea just how dangerous.

2

LUCA

Just when I thought tonight was going to be nothing but business.

"Boss?" Vinny nudges me, then jerks his chin toward the dark hallway leading back to my office. That's all he needs to say, with that one small gesture for me to get the message. There's a visitor waiting for me, and I shouldn't keep him waiting. Then again, maybe I should. I'll let him sweat a little, let him question the poor choices that have led him to this, the final night of his life. The stupid, sloppy bastard.

First, there was the matter of kissing a little ass at the VIP table. It was the last thing I felt like doing with a plaything waiting for me, but now I'm glad I made the sacrifice. Otherwise, I would never have bumped into this cute little piece of ass who thinks I don't know she deliberately fell against me. Somebody needs to tell her this isn't my first rodeo.

"In a minute," I tell Vinny before turning my attention back to her. She can't be more than a couple of inches above five feet, with a curvy little body and big blue eyes.

The sort of eyes a man could drown in if that's his thing. Her pouty lips draw my gaze, and already, I can imagine them wrapped around my cock, looking down at those blue eyes, listening as she chokes while I force myself against the back of her throat again and again. Would she cry while choking on my cock? I'm betting she would, a little thing like her.

So easy to control. My cock stiffens at the mere thought, and I clench my jaw, working it back and forth as I take a focusing breath.

"At least let me get you another drink." I look down at her glass, then down at the Armani jacket she carelessly splashed. "White wine?" Her head bobs up and down, and I wave Vinny toward the bar before hooking an arm around her tiny waist. "Come on. Let's sit down. Are you sure you're all right? You didn't twist or sprain anything?"

"I'm fine. Thank you, I feel so bad. I'm sure you're busy."

Yeah, busy inhaling the vanilla aroma coming off light brown hair I'm going to wrap around my fist later. "Never too busy to spend a few minutes with a beautiful woman," I say, guiding her into one of the booths and watching as she slides in gracefully, her dress hugging her curves, carving out a seductive silhouette.

"Oh, stop," she brushes me off, her cheeks glowing pink as she looks down at the table.

Sweet and innocent.

My favorite type.

Fuck knows, I've seen enough jaded, cynical bitches in my time. They might stir my dick, but they don't pique my interest.

Vinny comes over with the wine, which he places in front of her before taking a step backward, hands clasped in front of him. "You can go," I announce. "I'll meet you in a few." His brows lift over his narrowed eyes, but he shrugs it off, leaving us alone—as alone as you can be in a club where a few hundred people are dancing, drinking, and putting money in my family's pockets.

"What's your name?" I ask, leaning back against the leather cushion.

"Em," she replies with a soft smile.

Her eyes are a pair of sapphires on fire, burning their way into my skull, threatening to tear apart everything I'd planned for tonight. I shift in my seat once my wakening dick makes me uncomfortable. "It's nice to meet you."

"And what's your name?" she counters.

I let out a laugh, shaking my head, not buying it for a second. "Try again."

She shrugs, and I narrow my eyes. "You know who I am."

I've watched enough men realize they're not as bright as they think to recognize the doubt that passes over her heart-shaped face. It doesn't last long. "Santoro, right? You're one of the Santoros."

"That's right. But which one? Am I Dante, the older son with a stick up his ass?" I spread my arms to either side, across the top of the booth. "Or am I the younger, much more handsome and talented son?"

Her laughter lights up her face. "Wow. With a description like that, I don't really have to guess, do I?" Her sarcasm is heavy as she takes in the decor, toying with her glass. "This place is really cool. Is it hard to run a club?"

"Not when you hire the right people to manage things for you."

"Come on. Somebody like you..." she arches an eyebrow, and those lips I can't take my eyes off of curve in a knowing grin, "… you would hand the reins over to somebody else?"

I sense the challenge in her question, and damn if it doesn't make blood surge to my dick and stiffen it all at once. "I said I'd let them manage it," I remind her. "I didn't say they hold the reins. Only I do that."

Leaning in and thrusting her tits forward enticingly, she asks, "And does that go for every part of your life? Or just the club?"

Hunger, much deeper and stronger than anything I'm used to, stirs in my core and leaves me salivating, wanting to lunge over the table and take her. "I would love to show you personally," I offer, grunting helplessly when her cheeks flush and her eyes darken. Much more of this, and we're going to need a trip back to one of the private rooms.

As it is, I'm not sure I can last the rest of the night with an unrelenting hard-on. It's not a bad idea, either, relieving some tension before I settle business. She wouldn't resist, not with her tits heaving with every shallow, excited breath and those lips, full, parted, and begging for attention.

I turn to look over my shoulder toward the hall, where Vinny is standing in front. Anybody who takes a single glance at him knows better than to approach. He catches my eye and lifts his chin in a silent question. I fucking hate being reminded of work when I'm trying to have fun.

How many times do we have to go over this?

"I'm probably keeping you from something important, aren't I? I really am fine, Mr. Santoro." My name rolls off her tongue, and now I want her to say it again and again, preferably while I'm licking my way up the inside of her thighs.

I have to clench my fists under the table in an attempt to ward off the desire to reach out and test the softness of her skin and the fullness of those melon tits ready to spill over the top of her dress. It's extremely rare for anyone to suddenly hit me this hard with desire. Something about her calls out, sparking something in me I clearly have no control over.

And that's a problem.

If there's one thing I need at all times, it's control. I need to leave this table and forget she exists in favor of what has to be done tonight. I'm sure by the time my former best friend's body is being dragged from my office, I won't remember what I found so appealing about little Em, which is probably why I'm so reluctant to leave her.

"Do me a favor?" I ask with a grin, watching the way her lips touch the glass and she toys with the stem when she isn't sipping.

What could those fingers do to me?

"Depends on the favor," she teases with a smirk that stirs a growl in my chest.

"Stick around. I have a few things to settle, but I would very much like to continue our conversation later." I risk reaching across the table, letting the backs of my fingers glide over her knuckles. She sucks in the tiniest breath through her parted lips, and fuck, it does something to me. Something deep, dark, and needful begins to grow. "I'd like to get to know you better."

Her teeth sink into her lip before she nods. "I'll be here," she promises in a shaky voice.

I rise, lifting her hand to my lips, letting them linger against her smooth skin until a shiver runs through her body and into mine. I would swear it was real, that I didn't imagine it. "You better be," I warn. "I would hate to have to search the city for you." Her teeth sink into her juicy lip, and the sight makes me groan before I force myself to turn away.

I was planning on savoring Frankie's untimely but much-earned demise. I've been looking forward to it for the past week, ever since I received confirmation of him taking meetings with that son of a bitch, Vitali. He might as well be my brother—we're that close. *Were* that close. Past tense. Now, he's nothing more than another task to check off my list before I return to the woman who stole my attention.

Vinny steps aside so I can walk down the narrow hall and into my office, and it takes a second for me to adjust to the sudden change in atmosphere. The soundproof room doesn't allow anything to filter through the walls in either direction, taking me from a deafening roar to near silence, minus Frankie's pointless sobs. "Luca... please, man..."

He's where I left him, his wrists and ankles duct taped to the arms and legs of a chair placed square in the middle of a sheet of plastic covering the floor. The same plastic drapes over my desk and the furniture I would rather not soil with this degenerate blood. Bobby and Mike stand to either side of him, making sure he isn't going anywhere just in case a sudden burst of self-preservation lets him snap the tape.

"Do either of you hear something?" I ask the guys standing guard. "It almost sounds like a sniveling piece of shit trying to beg for mercy."

"Luca..." he groans out.

"A sniveling piece of shit who thinks it will make a difference if he whines and begs." I unbutton my wine-stained jacket, leaving it on the other side of the room before removing my cufflinks and slowly rolling up my sleeves. "A sniveling piece of shit who I now understand is the reason our last shipment to Sicily got detained by port authorities."

"Luca," the worthless sack of flesh I once considered family, continues.

"Shut the fuck up," I roar. In a flash, I'm across the room, taking a handful of his sweat-soaked hair and yanking hard until he's looking up into my eyes. He reeks of terror, not to mention piss. The stupid son of a bitch pissed himself. "Do not speak unless I ask you a question. You will not get through to me no matter how you try. You will not change my mind or erase the fucking heartbreak you put my family through. Do you realize the man who welcomed you at his table and gave you a bed to sleep in when your old man was beating the shit out of you on the daily didn't leave his room for two fucking days after he found out what you did?"

I shove his head away, then wipe my hand on his sleeve while snarling in disgust. "You broke my father's fucking heart. Do you think I would let you get away with that? Do you know me at all?"

"I'm sorry! I didn't have a choice!"

"Yeah, that's what they all say," I snort before crouching in front of him, reveling in the bruising that's already blackened both of his eyes, his cheekbone, and his jaw. The boys had a good time subduing him, and I wasn't about to hold them back. "What did they offer?"

"Man, it wasn't like that."

"Then tell me what it was like," I murmur. "Come on. You could always tell me anything, remember? Like that whore in Atlantic City who OD'd in your hotel bathroom. You told me about that, didn't you? When you needed my help."

He blurts out a sob and tries to look away. "Or what about that night on the parkway when you were coked out of your fucking mind and hit that car full of girls on their way back from a bachelorette party?" I whisper, watching him squirm in shame and soak up every last drop. "Remember that? The way their car flipped? Refresh my memory. How many of those girls ended up flying out of the car and skidding across the pavement until their skin peeled off? I'm a little rusty on the details."

"I needed the money!" he screams, shaking, tears and blood mixing as they run down his cheeks.

I close my eyes and take a deep breath in hopes of warding off the nausea gripping my stomach. After all we've experienced together, it boiled down to money. *"You know I love the kid, but he can't be trusted."* Papa's warning echoes in my head. How many times did I hear him say that? *"Frankie is a live wire, unpredictable, undisciplined."*

"For what? Gambling?" I ask, and his head bobs. "And you didn't come to me?"

"I couldn't. I *couldn't!*" he insists when I turn away. "You told me never again, man. And I guess... I don't know... they heard how much I owed. They paid it all off."

"How lucky for you. Now, you'll die debt-free."

"No." His pleas rise in pitch until they're more like shrieks. "No! Luca, we're fucking brothers!"

Brothers? The word leaves me shaking off a twinge of pain in my chest. "That's what I used to think." I run my hand over the array of tools resting on my plastic-covered desk. *Which to use?* "If anything, I should thank you."

"Wh-what? For what?"

"For reminding me of the dangers of letting someone get too close. It can blind a man, and I can't afford that. Better to lose a single shipment and have the lawyers work overtime than lose anything more precious."

I decide on the hammer and turn to him, testing the weight and balance in my hand while he moans and sobs and pleads. "All the love I felt for you has turned into disgust just as deep. Just as powerful."

"*Luca.*" My name is a plea, and I can almost hear the kid he used to be in his weak, heartfelt whimpering. "Please. I love you, man."

All I can do is offer a grim smile as I stop in front of where he sits and waits for the inevitable. "I know. And I loved you too."

With my eyes locked on his, I raise the hammer and get to work.

3

EMILIA

How is everybody else in the club going through the motions of a night out when I'm sitting here, utterly certain a storm has swept over me? My hand is still tingling in the moments after Luca Santoro touched his lips to it. It ran through my body and lit up the darkest places until I was still breathless and too shaky to get out of the booth after he left.

What did the man do to me? A simple kiss on my hand, and I'm swooning?

"What the fuck are you thinking?" Craig's accusatory voice barely pulls me out of the trance Luca left me in before his hand closes around my arm. Suddenly, he's hauling me out of the booth and practically carrying me to the front of the club, close to the entrance.

"Get off me!" I snap, yanking my arm from his grasp and quickly looking around. "Way to go. Cause a scene and blow my cover."

His head snaps back as if I slapped him, which I wish I had. "Blow your *cover?* What do you think this is, a cop show on TV?" He jerks his thumb in the direction of the booth he unceremoniously yanked me from. "What are you doing, flirting with that asshole?"

I sincerely hope for both our sakes that this looks like a fight between a couple rather than what it really is. "What do you think?"

"Honestly, I don't have the faintest idea. What do you hope to accomplish? Flashing your tits isn't going to get you anywhere. Not this time," he states like he has any idea.

It's my turn to react in surprise, gasping before squaring my shoulders to face him. "What does that mean?"

He knows he made a mistake. Scrubbing a hand over the top of his head, he then rakes back his thinning sandy-blond hair before blowing out a sigh, his large belly expanding. "Forget I said it."

"Like hell. Talk. Do you want to be a big man? Go ahead." I fold my arms, which I know draws attention to the tits he's so concerned about me flashing around. "Because you're not going to say anything I haven't already heard. A twenty-four-year-old couldn't possibly pass the exam without blowing a few guys along the way, right? Maybe I let them touch my tits? Slide their dick up in between them and—"

"Enough," he snaps, curling his lip in a disgusted sneer.

"No. You don't get to act disgusted when you were the one who brought it up. Sorry if you and your buddies can't possibly accept that I got where I am through hard work." Snorting, I nod to the empty glass he's holding. "Why don't you have another drink to make yourself feel better?"

He lowers his brow. "Bitch."

"Asshole."

At least we're finally being honest with each other.

"You know what? Waste your time here. Be my guest.

And find your own damn way home while you're at it because I'm sick of wasting my time on your bullshit hunches."

I would tell him to wait, but I don't want him to. I didn't want him around tonight, anyway. I only mentioned my plan to him as a professional courtesy and the fact that if I found anything tonight, I didn't want to hear a bunch of crap afterward about how I didn't give him the heads-up I was going to the club.

It takes me a while, standing with my back against the wall, fighting to control myself. That pig. I always knew Craig was one, and I had a feeling he resented me being not only a girl but also ten years younger than him. I just didn't think he'd go so far as to accuse me of sleeping my way into a detective position.

My pulse is still a little faster than it should be by the time I gather myself enough to push away from the wall, but then thoughts of Luca Santoro aren't helping. I've never met anybody like him. I figured charm, as well as clever and sly, would be part of it. Somebody who has managed to evade law enforcement his entire life would have to be charming. That's how he gets what he wants.

But it's one thing to know the Empire State Building is tall and another to stand at the top and look down over the city. That's how I felt in his presence—a little dizzy from being so high up, slightly disoriented. Exhilarated. He did that to me, and all it took was a few minutes together at a table and the briefest touch of his fingers and lips against my skin.

I can only imagine how it would feel if he put his lips in other places.

This is why I don't typically drink. A single glass of wine has me thinking ridiculous thoughts.

What do I do now? Drink some water, definitely, but then

what? Do I stick around? *Do I leave?* There's a good chance he'll forget about me while he's doing whatever it was that was so important, and that deduction has my gaze landing on the narrow hallway where he disappeared down.

My detective instincts kick in, and I instantly question where it leads. The man who shadows him, what does he know? I square my shoulders and fold my arms across my chest, wondering what he's doing right now. What business distracted him and pulled him away from me? That matters a lot more than a pair of slightly moist panties and the warmth still blazing between my thighs when I recall the electricity that flowed between us when he met my gaze over the top of my hand.

It has to be the wine playing tricks on me.

I make it a point to move around the club after grabbing a bottle of water from the bar, but my attention is always on that ominous dark hall and the giant of a man, Vinny, blocking it. I catch his eye once or twice, but he seems unimpressed and uninterested, always turning straight ahead while wearing a stony expression. That's for the best. I don't want him to remember me after...

After what?

There's one thing Craig was right about. Aside from trying to get a look at Luca and how he does business, I have no idea what I'm doing here. It all seems to be above board from what I've seen so far. Something tells me the bad stuff happens in his office or whatever is behind the door.

I have to build this case. Captain Dougherty is counting on me, for one thing. I practically begged to be put on this case. I was desperate to prove myself.

I still am.

But is coming around here and putting myself in

Luca's path the same as the sort of clichéd bullshit jealousy Craig accused me of? Maybe I'm no better than he thinks, which is why I have to find something. Anything. The first in a long line of dominoes. All it takes is the first one to fall.

Vinny disappears down the hall. *Interesting.* I wait five minutes, then ten, but he doesn't return. Neither does Luca. I wonder what's happening in there that could be important enough for him to leave the hall unguarded after hovering for so long.

I'm already walking toward it before I know what I'm doing. That seems to be the way things are going tonight. I'm usually so methodical in everything I do, thriving on the chaos and noticing every little detail surrounding me, but tonight, I keep acting without thinking. I don't know if it's Luca or my own determination to find something. Something to prove my worth.

This is crazy. I shouldn't do this. That's the only bit of common sense that filters through my mind before I duck down the hall and head straight for the only door at the far end.

Testing the knob, I hold my breath.

It turns.

Here goes nothing. Before I can talk out of it, I ease the door open while pretending to stumble inside drunkenly like I'm trying to be provocative. "I couldn't wait for you another minute—"

It comes to me in flashes like I'm looking at pictures after the fact.

Plastic sheets covering everything.

Red. Splattered everywhere. *Blood.* The coppery tang fills my nostrils all at once.

The man holding a blood-coated hammer, letting it hang at his side.

Tap, tap, tap. The blood drips from the end onto the plastic.

In a chair sits what might have been a man but is now a broken, blood-soaked lump of flesh.

I joined the force straight out of high school. I always knew exactly what I wanted to do. It only took six years to become a detective. I've seen a lot of things—too many things. But that was always after the fact.

It was never *during*.

And the victim was never gurgling, choking weakly on their own blood when I found them. *He's still alive.* I can't recognize anything close to a human face under all that blood, but somehow, he's still breathing.

The man with the hammer spins with a surprised grunt, and I knew, didn't I? I knew who he was before I stepped foot in this club. I knew what he was capable of and what he had probably done.

The sight of Luca Santoro's blood-spattered face steals my breath and makes the world spin. Before I can allow my extensive training to kick in, my legs go out, and pain explodes in my head before everything goes black.

4

LUCA

re you fucking kidding me?

"What the fuck, Vin?" I hiss as my braindead bodyguard pulls Em the rest of the way into the room and slams the door. This time, he locks it. "What were you thinking?"

"Sorry, boss."

"You think I fucking care if you're sorry? Anybody could've walked in here!" My heart's racing, and my adrenaline is still pumping. I'm in a dangerous place—clearheaded enough to see what's happening to my body and my brain but not enough to give a shit. Blood roars in my ears, and my chest heaves like I've come back from battle, blood-soaked and victorious.

This is not the time to fuck with me.

"I should use this fucking hammer on you," I growl out. "How did you forget something so simple as locking the damn door? I cannot believe you did that."

He absorbs my rage without looking at me. Instead, he picks her up with no effort and drapes her across the plastic-covered leather couch. "I think her head's bleeding," Vinny offers as if the sight of blood isn't enough to confirm that.

Another wonderful development. "Just leave her there. I'll figure something out as soon as I'm finished dealing with this problem."

A problem that has gone silent. Fuck. He died when I wasn't looking. I was hoping to witness those final breaths so I could burn the image in my memory and recall it every time I'm on the verge of trusting an outsider from now until the day I die.

"Get rid of him." I drop the hammer on the floor, knowing it will be taken away with the body and the plastic, disposed of in the same barrel of acid as Frankie's body. Normally, I would have him dismembered, maybe leave a few pieces around where part of my victim's crew could find them.

A message, in other words.

"Careful with the corpse. We don't want Vitali getting the heads-up yet that we know he was behind the port fiasco." My father's words echo in my mind. As if he needed to remind me, like this is my first fucking day on the job.

Now, there's the matter of cleaning myself up before she regains consciousness. There might still be a chance to convince her she saw nothing, but there's no hope if she sees me the way I am now.

The attached full bath and dressing room come in handy at a time like this. Stripping down to my underwear, I bundle the suit in another wad of plastic before handing it off to Mike, one of the men in the room.

"What are you doing?" I ask Vinny, who hovers at Em's side. "Get back out there. We don't want anybody else trying to sneak their way in," I snap, knowing he would rather be anywhere but here. When I am as pissed as I am now, I don't need a hammer to do damage, and he knows it.

Once I've scrubbed my hands clean with a nail brush and soap, I pull the plastic from beneath Em's limp body, then open her purse. Her driver's license sits outside her wallet, and I see she wasn't necessarily lying about her name. Em, short for Emilia Washington, twenty-four years old. She lives in what I immediately recognize as a shitty part of Brooklyn. She can't feel safe in that environment, someone as tiny and defenseless as she is.

What the fuck was she doing coming in here? She said she knows who I am, knows my family. Yet she would stroll in here the way she did? Something doesn't add up. Maybe she downed a few shots after I left her.

Trying to process her intentions, I'm almost oblivious to Mike and Bobby carrying the corpse through the back door and into a waiting van in the alley. As soon as the door clicks shut, I open her wallet, glad they're out of the room. For some reason, I just know I can't let them witness my reaction to what I find.

"A detective?" NYPD-issued ID, Detective Emilia Washington. My hands shake, and everything goes red.

This lying cunt.

No fucking way is this a coincidence. She didn't wander into the club tonight, looking for a good time. She had a purpose. *Me.* I knew that little stumbling act she pulled earlier was just that. An act. I didn't guess how far it went.

"Yo, boss, we're out of here." Bobby steps inside, takes one more look around, and nods in satisfaction.

No one would ever know what went on tonight. That is, not unless they took a look at me in my current state, stripped down to my underwear with rust-colored stains on my skin where the blood soaked through.

"Yeah, go ahead. Update me when it's over," I rattle off, operating on autopilot, practically flying blind while I grope around in my head for an answer to a question I haven't yet asked. *What do I do next?*

She's still out cold, so I take advantage by running my hands over her lush body to look for a wire. Minutes ago, the prospect of fondling her had my cock straining. Now, the act of touching her makes my stomach churn. A cop. A fucking cop flirting with me.

She's clean, and so is the purse, nothing hidden in the lining. Returning everything to its rightful place so it doesn't look like I rummaged through her bag, I don't know my play yet. Whatever it is, I have to tread carefully. If my father or even Dante knew I had an unconscious detective at my mercy, they would be here in an instant, taking pleasure in skinning her alive, limb by gorgeous limb.

With one eye on her, I return to the bathroom, where I can see her through the glass shower door. I scrub myself down quickly and efficiently, my eyes trained on her. Frankie's blood swirls down the drain, and I suppose part of me ought to be grateful for this unexpected distraction. I don't have to reflect on the fact that I brutally murdered my lifelong best friend minutes ago.

I could murder her now, and no one would know. I could put that cute little body in another barrel of acid and dissolve her until she's nothing but sludge. Let the NYPD figure out what to make of that.

That's what I *should* do.

As much as the idea makes my blood race, I'm self-aware enough to know that would never work. I didn't see anybody with her in the short time we spent together, but there's a chance somebody knew she was coming here tonight. It would take too much work to erase her presence from the club to make the endeavor worth it. Deleting video footage, making sure she didn't leave her credit card at the bar to run a tab... I don't have the time for that. And I doubt Papa or Dante would appreciate the headache if the cops came sniffing around.

I can't let her leave, though. She saw too much. Everything. Those baby blues took in the aftermath of my sense of betrayal. She saw Frankie's blood-soaked body and heard him gurgle on his blood.

She saw me. She looked me straight in the eye.

By the time I step out of the shower and dry off, she still hasn't moved. How do I navigate this? I could tell her I know everything. Come to think of it, she might not be a bad resource to have on the inside. She lives in a shitty part of the city and can't make much as a detective, not enough to give her security in this economy. I might not be one of the so-called regular people, but I know that much. I could make her an offer and convince her to work together.

I have more than money to offer. She liked me. She wanted me. I could practically smell it on her, in the air, and taste it on her skin when I kissed her hand. She would melt like butter under the right touch. And what a game it could be. Getting my dick wet and protecting what's mine at the same time.

There's a reason I keep identical suits in my closet. I've already been seen in my ruined one tonight. Showing up at the bar wearing something different might catch someone's attention. I can't afford not to be too careful, especially when so many mistakes have already been made. Letting her see me in a different suit would be the same as a confession. She has no proof, though. I have to remind myself of that when the impulse to strangle her threatens to consume me.

This fucking bitch. Anger claws its way up my spine, settling like a weight across my shoulder blades.

I replace my cufflinks, staring down at her while I do. There is a trace of blood behind her ear, but she can't have done much damage since head wounds tend to bleed more than any other. Frankie's sure as hell did.

She thought she could stroll in here, seduce me, and work her way into my business. A detective at twenty-four. Who the hell does that? Especially a girl who could easily pass for sixteen. She's probably the kid who reminded the teacher on Friday afternoon that she forgot to assign homework. She wanted to be a hero. She thinks she'll shoot to the top of the ladder before she turns thirty. Commissioner Washington.

Not at my expense, she won't.

It's another long, torturous ten minutes or so before she stirs. By now, I'm behind my desk, trying to work on my laptop while watching her.

But I'm on one knee at her side when she opens her eyes and blinks fast. "There you are," I whisper, brushing hair away from her cheeks and watching as she begins breathing faster. She remembers.

Fuck.

"What…" She flinches away from my touch while her eyes dart around the room. "What happened?"

"You fell. You came in here, and you were mumbling about something or other. I couldn't catch it. Then you must've tripped in those ridiculous shoes because the next thing I knew, you were unconscious on the floor. You really should rethink your choice of footwear when you go out. That's twice tonight you've stumbled, and I wasn't there to catch you this time," I explain, ensuring everything is plausible.

I can almost taste her confusion. Her apprehension.

Her panicked pulse flutters in her slim throat as she sits up. Her eyes dart here, there, all over the room. She's looking for evidence of what she saw. Trying to understand how everything is suddenly so different.

"Say something," I urge in a voice that in no way conveys the bubbling rage in my chest. It's tight, almost to the point I can't breathe, but she can't know that. She has to believe I'm sincere.

"I'm sorry," she mumbles, trembling, trying to fight it and failing. I see it in the way she clenches her jaw and tightens her fists in her lap. "I shouldn't have walked in like that. I was trying to…" Her words die off, and I know exactly what the bitch was trying to do.

As it turns out, the past week of pretending nothing was wrong between Frankie and me was perfect training for this moment. I can smile when all I want to do is snap her neck. "I get it. You wouldn't be the first woman to walk in here when she saw an opportunity. But you are the only one I would hate having to throw out."

Her lips twitch. "Thanks. Was there somebody else in here? When I came in? Everything looks…"

Either she is genuinely concussed, or she's overplaying her hand. I'm hoping it's the former rather than the latter. "Vinny was here. You met him outside. That's it."

I use a finger to lift her dark hair and examine her head. "You really did a number on yourself. Maybe we should take you to the hospital and get you checked out," I offer.

"No," she blurts out, eyes wide as if she senses danger. She's not so concussed that she can't understand how potentially fatal that would be. "No, thank you. I… couldn't afford it, anyway. You know how it is." I'll give it to her. She can still think fast.

Unfortunately, it's not looking good for me—or her.

She's sexy and intelligent, a lethal combination and a headache if I were to go there, regardless of the way her smooth skin beckons my touch.

"I'd be more than happy to cover it," I offer in a warm voice, needing to lay it on thick. Be overly caring, almost smothering. Anything to throw her off track.

"No, thank you. Really."

To think I was imagining her in my bed earlier. That was her plan. Dressing like a slut, coming in here and batting those eyelashes at me. And I was the stupid fuck who fell for it. "As long as you're sure. Do you want to maybe lie down a little while longer? Make sure you're all right?" I question, keeping up the façade that I give a shit.

"No. No, I don't think so," Emilia dismisses, looking around wildly, her hands sliding over the sofa before she closes one around her bag. "I better go. I'm sure I'll feel better in the morning."

"You know, they say it's not safe to sleep if you have a concussion."

"I'm sure I'll be fine."

"Do you have someone at home to take care of you, just in case?" I didn't count on my enjoyment of her squirming anxiety. Not so tough when she's on her own, one-on-one with a man she knows is a murderer. This was not the night for her to go out unarmed.

She stiffens her spine while her jaw tightens, and for one exhilarating moment, I know she's about to drop the act and tell me to fuck off. I almost wish she would, so I could too. Yet she pulls back at the last second and forces a faint smile. "Uh... sure. I will really be fine. Thank you."

"Nothing to thank me for. I gave you somewhere to rest, that's all." I help her stand, running my thumbs over her knuckles and pretending not to notice how cold and sweaty her palms are. "I could have my driver take you home."

Out of everything I've suggested so far, that appeals to her the least. "No! No, really. I'll be fine." She withdraws her hands from mine and pulls out her phone. "I'm going to get an Uber."

Another potential trap. She could've ubered here. There would've been a record of her arrival. Learning this, I know I made the right decision, letting her live.

"Good idea. I wouldn't want you driving," I offer, not realizing I had this level of self-control. Enough that it allows me to run a hand down her arm without snapping it like a twig.

A fucking detective.

This lying bitch.

Her fear radiates from her eyes when they meet mine.

She needs to pay for this. I'm going to find a way to make her pay for fucking with me, if not tonight, then soon. That's a promise.

"It was a real pleasure meeting you," I utter in a velvet voice that could temper chocolate. I have to visualize the pleasure of terrorizing Emilia to make my smile seem genuine and my touch gentle when I take her by her shoulders and pull her in. She doesn't have time to gasp and stiffen before I crush my lips against hers. Sweet, plump, firm. I part them with my tongue and invade her mouth, kissing her with everything I have, relishing the touch of her body to mine when there's no choice but to melt against me.

This isn't about anything more than undoing her, fucking with her head, yet my cock didn't get the memo. It twitches and grows before going stiff when she whimpers helplessly into my mouth.

Her legs are sagging by the time I let her up for air, and

her gaze is soft and unfocused when I pull away. "I hope I can see you again soon," I croon, wiping a bit of smudged lipstick away from the corner of her mouth with my thumb before releasing her.

"I... hope so... too," she stammers out, then flees the room as though it's on fire, almost falling against the door before opening it and flinging herself through.

Some brave detective. She has no idea what she's gotten herself into.

Make no mistake, it's something I won't let her forget.

5

EMILIA

When Monday morning comes, it brings a lump in my chest that only gets bigger the closer I get to the station. Craig was out of town all weekend, and having two days without the possibility of running into him was a gift. With the way we left things on Friday night, it was good for us to cool off a little.

And I needed the time to get my head together too, even if I don't feel like that's been achieved by the time I walk into the station. Per our usual custom, it's my turn to grab coffee, so I reach my desk in our shared office, balancing a pair of steaming lattes in a cardboard carrier.

Craig already arrived, and he turns away from the work I compiled over the weekend to accept his latte, grunting. "Look who's been a busy girl while I was out of town."

"How was the weekend?" I ask because I will not entertain his bullshit today. I can't. There's too much to be done to play childish games.

"I spent the whole time pretending to give a shit about

a bunch of ten-year-olds playing soccer in a tournament my kid's team didn't win. It was joyful."

"Sorry to hear that."

"So?" he prods in his arrogant way while I slide out of my jacket. "Are you going to answer my question?"

"You didn't ask a question." I stand back with my drink while he studies the photos I printed out and the profiles I put together on the Santoro and Vitali families.

"Is there any ink left in the printer after all this?" he asks with a sarcastic snort that gets my blood simmering.

Why not pat me on the head and patronize me a little harder?

"I'm sure it'll be fine," I grit out.

"It's been a busy weekend for them," he muses, looking at one photo after another. "As I'm sure you know."

Know? I've visited the crime scenes. "Things are ramping up. A shoot-out in front of a Vitali bar on Saturday, a drive-by yesterday on Santoro turf. It's getting uglier."

"Word has it, old man Vitali is on his last legs, so yeah, everybody's trying to carve up what they can with the family perceived as being weak." He turns to me, arching an eyebrow.

Clearly, the part of our day where we talk about things we already know in order to ease the tension between us is over—kind of the way a couple will reconnect after a fight using common ground, like adding something to a grocery list or asking who last let the dog outside. "I shouldn't have said what I said when we were out on Friday. There was no excuse for it."

"You're right. There was no excuse," I agree.

Heaving a sigh, he perches at the edge of my desk with his back to the corkboard I spent all weekend filling. "Here's the thing you need to hear, though I know you don't want to hear it."

Here we go. I need to brace myself.

"You can't go charging headfirst into everything. I know you've had it pretty easy so far." When I suck in a breath, prepared to fight, he holds up a hand and shakes his head. "Let me finish before you get all up in your feelings. I'm sure you worked hard, but there are lots of people who work twice as hard and never get as far as you already have. You're on the fast track. But you're going to come up against a situation one day where the waters don't magically part for you to walk through. Do you understand what I'm trying to say? You could end up getting yourself into serious trouble, strutting around with all this bravado. It's no good. Don't do that to yourself."

As if the waters have ever magically parted for me. I want to say that to him, but instead, I settle for, "Point taken."

He rolls his eyes. "Thank you is the response you were looking for. Why is that so much to ask?" he challenges, and I have to force myself to count to five in my head before I say something I'll regret.

The thing is, I would never admit this to him with a gun to my head that I know he's right. How do I know? Because I may have committed an unforgivable mistake on Friday night. Really, there's no *might* about it. I know I did. And I spent the weekend doing penance, working until my eyes burned and my head ached, digging deep into the families, trying to get to the root of their feud.

Increased activity on the streets heightens my sense of urgency. So far, only members of the respective crews were taken out this weekend. How long will that be the case? When are innocent bystanders going to be caught in the middle?

How long are they going to keep getting away with it?

For as long as men like Luca Santoro keep using their charm to skate their way through everything.

Because I'm sure that's what he did to me on Friday with his velvety voice and hypnotic eyes. He did his best to convince me I didn't see anything out of the ordinary in that room, but I know that's not true. Even if I don't have proof and everything is still a little fuzzy, I've been popping aspirin like it's my job in the days since, thanks to the bump at the base of my skull. There is no way I hit my head hard enough to make up something that grotesque.

The image of that beaten, dying man is burned into my memory. Luca used a hammer to break his face apart and not only his face. The guy's fingers were bent at odd angles like that's where Luca had started before working his way into the truly horrific stages. Why would he take that kind of a risk? All I had to do was step through an unlocked door, and bam, there it was. And a man like him would never take that kind of risk.

Would he? Or has he been doing it for so long it never occurred to him he might not get away with it?

Maybe I am making it all up.

Maybe it doesn't make sense because it didn't happen the way I remember it.

I could be taking my feelings about his family and their history and concocting a gruesome but false memory. It happens all the time.

But it doesn't happen to me.

One thing I know for sure is that, if nothing else, I'm not telling Craig. That sort of admission would be like opening Pandora's box. He would never let me live it down, especially if he found out how long I laid there unconscious in a room where Luca could've done anything to me while I was out. He could have even searched through my bag and found my badge. *No.* He would have killed me on the spot, but I was here and very much alive.

Right on cue, a shiver runs through me at the mere suggestion of the man whose kiss is seared in my memory. I've never been so surprised. At first, I was repulsed. But not for long. Some things are stronger than principles, and his kiss qualified. I was no match for its power and dominance.

I'm a detective. I've made it my mission to put an end to that man and his family and all of the pain and senseless loss they've caused. I have no business getting flustered over him, no matter how skilled he is with his lips and tongue.

"Are you listening to me?" Craig snaps fingers close to my face, something he knows I detest. "I asked if anything else happened that night. Did you leave soon after, or did you stick around?"

"I left after another half hour or so."

"Did you see Luca or anybody else?"

Shaking my head, I lift my cup to my lips and hope it helps hide any guilt that might show up on my face. "No," I report after swallowing. "He never came back."

What are you doing? Protecting him? I push the idea away just as far as it can go. I would never protect Luca or any of his kind. It's called self-preservation. I can't exactly go around accusing someone of murder when I have no proof whatsoever. I don't know who was in the chair—if anyone was there in the first place.

As if I didn't have enough reason to hate Luca before now, he's made me question myself. He's planted doubt, and that is not something I can afford.

"All's well that ends well," he offers, and I'm glad he feels that way.

I, on the other hand, wonder if this weekend's

increased activity had anything to do with the man who may or may not have been brutally beaten to death on Friday night.

A THIN, cold drizzle hits my shoulders and the hood of my jacket once I step out of the corner store with a bag of groceries. The gray skies and dampness don't do much for my already dark mood, but they encourage me to hustle my way down the street, my head ducked, shoulders hunched against the light but incessant onslaught of raindrops. A small, soaked cat hides beneath the sparse shelter of a trash can lid propped against the side of the can, and I wish I had something to give it to eat, but I doubt frozen pizza and ice cream is its preferred diet.

This is the sort of day junk food reigns supreme. Not that I've ever been accused of being the healthiest eater. Whatever is quickest is what I usually settle on. Besides, why go to all the trouble of fixing a big meal for only myself?

I don't like using the hood of my jacket since it limits my peripheral vision. My nerves are on edge, and I'm too jumpy, suspicious of every man I pass. They're only people like me trying to get home where it's dry and warm, yet something in my head wants to identify them as a threat. More than once, I turn to glance over my shoulder when the hair on the back of my neck lifts in a warning.

I really fucked myself over, didn't I? The man got in my head and put down roots. Spending the weekend looking into his background didn't exactly help things, either. He's been on my mind, front and center. Is it any wonder I'm jumpy as I duck into my building?

"That you, Emilia?" I briefly close my eyes and have to

draw a steadying breath at the sound of my neighbor's voice once I climb the three floors to my apartment. Ours are the only two currently inhabited out of the four on this floor. She's nice enough but lonely and doesn't have much to occupy her time. I know it makes her feel good having a detective living next door. And I would swear she sits by her door and waits for me to come home.

She opens the door as far as the chain lock will allow, and I give her a little wave. "Hi, Mrs. Henderson. Yes, it's me, just getting home."

"What about this weather, huh? It has been raining nonstop since yesterday afternoon."

"Yeah, but I'm sure we need it." Because isn't that what people always say at times like this?

"Anyway," she continues while the bag I'm carrying gets heavier every second. "I'm surprised you were out."

"What do you mean?"

"Your TV was on this morning. I figured you were home sick or took the day off for once."

"My TV?" I look toward my door, which is closed like I left it this morning.

"Yeah, and it was loud too. Playing some game show."

"I'm sorry if I bothered you. Maybe there's something wrong with it," I mumble, my tone uncertain.

"Could be. Who knows nowadays, right? Back in my day, you had a big set with a tube and got up to change the channels. Sometimes, I wish we could go back to that," she shares, but I honestly just want to go home and check things out.

"Well, I better put these things in the freezer."

She lets me go without any fuss, closing her door while I unlock mine. There's no sign of tampering, nothing broken, no scuff marks or scratches. Still, once I have the door open, I don't step into the apartment right away. I wait, watching, listening, expecting someone to jump out at me.

Someone with Luca's face.

Get over it. He's not some omnipresent bogeyman. I doubt he remembers I exist. Just some idiot who walked into his office unannounced, one of many women whose throat he's stuck his tongue down. Still, I hesitate before removing my holster and hanging it from the coat rack by the front door. I've never questioned whether I need to be armed in my own apartment... until now.

The television is just as I left it, which gives me hope Mrs. Henderson was hearing things. Sometimes, I think my neighbor makes things up as an excuse to have something to talk about. What a shame she has to freak me out in the process of finding a little human contact.

It isn't until I've preheated the oven and popped the pizza inside that I notice the tea kettle sitting on a different burner than the one I left it on this morning. I always use the bottom left of the four burners, then leave the kettle on the bottom right burner once I'm finished.

So why is it sitting on the back left, then? Doubt leaves my skin pebbled with goose bumps before I shake it off. I'm looking for reasons to be freaked out, scaring myself for no reason. I was in a hurry, so I used a different burner. Big deal.

Then why is the television remote on the arm of the couch instead of on the coffee table where I always leave it? I stand and stare at it as though I expect it to jump out and snap at me. I know I left the remote on the coffee table after I turned off the news and left for the station. I distinctly remember doing it.

Now, my lungs don't seem to want to fill with air. I turn in a slow circle, scrutinizing everything around me.

Maybe Mrs. Henderson wasn't imagining things.

Maybe somebody did break into my apartment today.

I dart over to the coat rack and withdraw my gun from the holster. Flipping off the safety, I begin a more deliberate search of my home. Not that it takes long, going through a one-bedroom apartment, but I check the closets, behind the shower curtain, and beneath my bed. Anywhere someone could lie in wait.

When my search yields nothing, I kneel beside the bed, wondering if I'm completely losing it. Did I really make it this easy for Luca to plant himself in my brain? I'm supposed to be above this. A professional. Yet I'm on my hands and knees, looking under the bed as if I'm a child, making sure nobody is ready to jump out and grab their ankle when they go to sleep. "Get it together," I whisper to myself, heading to the kitchen when the timer goes off, signaling dinner is ready.

Only I'm not so hungry anymore. Knowing I should still eat, I do it while standing by the window overlooking the street, pairing the pizza with one glass of red wine that quickly becomes two in hopes of calming my nerves. It'll knock my normally non-drinking ass out.

As I watch the city below, there's nothing inherently threatening about the rain-soaked pavement or the people hurrying along it in hopes of reaching shelter, but that doesn't stop me from gulping wine to soothe myself.

And it doesn't stop me from tucking my gun under the pillow before going to sleep.

Just in case.

Dante: *Check in.*

Dante: *I mean it.*

Dante: *Where the fuck are you, Luca? Don't make me send people looking around. Don't make me waste time.*

Fuck. Grinding my teeth, I respond to my older brother's most recent text.

Me: *Relax. Doing some work. I'm safe.*

Because I know what has him freaked. Losing three of our own yesterday—soldiers, low-level—but they were conducting business on the family's behalf when they were gunned down by some fucking coward in a passing car.

There's a reason I have a loaded gun in my lap. I'm not taking any fucking chances.

Which is why I happen to be where I am now, sitting in my car, watching the front windows of Emilia Washington's apartment. A shithole, nothing more. Pretty much exactly the way I imagined it when I learned the address.

"What are you doing up there?" I wonder out loud as I

watch her shadow dance across the ceiling. "Did you appreciate the presents I left?"

A few little things. Nothing major. Just enough to make Emilia question her surroundings and wonder if she got herself into more trouble than she counted on when she chose to screw with me. I like to think of it as a marinade. I'm getting her nice and tender for when I decide to renew our acquaintance.

Usually, I leave the breaking and entering to my soldiers, but I couldn't take a chance with her. No. A little stalking was necessary to uncover more about the detective who came to screw with me. But upon entering her bedroom, it's clear that work was her life. The space is neat and simple, with a tidy bed, crisp white sheets, and a desk piled with work stuff.

There weren't any personal decorations except for a picture of her with an older couple, I'm guessing, her family. But when I searched her drawers, closet, and personal belongings, there was no sign of a man anywhere. I couldn't help but feel a bit turned-on by the absence of a boyfriend. Good thing too, because I might have taken pleasure in gutting that fucker.

I wondered when the last time someone licked her pussy or made her moan out their name. Or those delicious lips, the same lips that left their mark on mine, were wrapped around a huge cock.

The light goes out, and I sit up straighter, anticipation making my heart race. She's going to bed. How long will it take her to fall asleep?

My phone beeps, and reluctantly, I peel my eyes away from her.

Dante: *We've got shit to discuss. Come home and meet me in the study.*

I let out a groan. He's always been an insufferable,

demanding jerk. Nothing has changed since those early days as kids. Our differences were like fire and ice, constantly clashing and never finding common ground. He expected me to jump whenever he called because he was the eldest. And now, it was just another example that made my teeth clench with anger.

Demanding I meet him in the study of the family home—the heart of the Long Island compound my family has owned for generations, surrounded by high, thick stone walls and always guarded, day and night. Over the years, Papa built smaller homes on the property for those of us old enough to be on our own but not old enough to be beyond his grasp.

If I had a dollar for every time he ordered me around.

It's better to let it go than to remind Dante I've got shit going on too. I'm well aware of the challenges we're facing right now. Maybe more aware than most, since so far, I'm the one who lost someone they once loved like a brother.

I doubt the Vitali had to try hard to steer Frankie to their side. He would've been desperate to get that money and clear his debts. They didn't do it because it was easy, though. They did it because they knew what it would mean for the betrayal to come from him. I feel it in my bones as I stare at the third-floor apartment window.

As far as I know from my intel within the NYPD, nothing has been reported about what she saw that night. Nobody whispering, nothing. Silence. I had a feeling she would play it smart and keep her mouth shut. Not out of self-preservation, either, but because she has no evidence. A girl who makes detective at twenty-four can't afford to make baseless accusations.

I wasn't born yesterday. While my family has never exactly colored within the lines of the law, we also know a lot about it. We have to if we want to do business and avoid prison.

As I take in the apartment above, I can imagine her dressed in one of the pajama sets I found today in her dresser. I picture her crawling into bed beneath what appears to be a handmade quilt, all alone in the dark. Wondering if the Big Bad Wolf is going to huff and puff his way back into her life.

Sitting here, one song after another plays soft and low, but I barely hear a note. And while I stare up at the front windows of Emilia's apartment, I envision her limp, almost lifeless body on my sofa, h er smiling and blushing from across the table, then gazing up at me, all hazy, confused, and flushed after the kiss.

I could go for another one of those.

More than one.

It's an hour before my resolve breaks. I shouldn't do this, take this sort of risk, but then I've never been good at playing it safe. I cross the street, my nose wrinkling at the stench of rotting leaves and wet garbage. How the fuck can she live here? Things don't get much better once I've stepped into the vestibule, which reeks of mouse shit and piss. If I were her and somebody offered to pay me for my discretion, I would jump at the opportunity—anything to get out of this dump.

My footsteps are quiet as I jog to the third floor, then round the post and walk down the narrow hall. It takes nothing to pick the locks. They're old and flimsy and definitely not up to the standards of a detective. Does she think she's invincible? Hell, I know the answer to that already. Only somebody who truly thinks they're one of the lucky ones would take the kinds of risks she does. I'm amazed she hasn't made herself a name in my family, come to think of it. It's shocking we don't already know about her.

As of this moment, only I do. And I prefer to keep it that way. She belongs only to me.

I pause in the living room, listening hard after passing the narrow kitchen. The bedsprings are creaky. I tested them myself so I would know if she moved. Since the only sound coming from her bedroom is soft snoring, I think I'm in good shape as I tiptoe to her room. She's the wild obsession I've developed over the past couple of days, and I'm a kid who just found his new favorite toy and can't be convinced to bother with boring things such as chores and homework.

This foolish girl. Thinking she's safe, that she can go rogue and trick her way into catching my attention, then what? Win the day? Be the heroine who took down Luca Santoro? It would take a hell of a lot more than her. Many have tried.

The bedroom door is open, making it easier for me to watch her sleep. At the first sight of her, my breath catches. This is as close as I've been to her since Friday, and the sudden proximity combined with her pure, angelic beauty is almost enough to buckle my knees. She's right there, mine for the taking. I wouldn't have to try. I could have her any way I wanted.

When I remember how quickly she melted against me, I doubt she would fight very hard, not once she realizes she's never had a real man. That no man ever touched, caressed, claimed her the way I would.

Not only is there no evidence of a man anywhere in this apartment, but there's a lack of male presence on her social media accounts. No vacations with a boyfriend, no cozy pictures in front of a Christmas tree. As far as I can tell, she's chronically single. Married to her work, if I had to guess.

What a waste.

Need bubbles in my core when Emilia shifts, throwing an arm over her head. It's almost enough to draw her tits out from under the thin tank top she's wearing. Her nipples are practically playing peekaboo, flirting with the neckline. I shudder when I imagine drawing them between my lips, flicking and sucking, grazing them with my teeth until she writhes and undulates, begging for more. How I would undo her and make her question everything she ever thought she knew.

The way she almost does to me. I can barely recognize myself as I take one soft, quiet step after another further into the room. I can't look away as I round the bed, aware of every twitch of the muscles in her face, the way her delicate brows draw together.

What is she dreaming of? Me? Frankie, or what was left of him by the time she stumbled into the room?

I pull open the dresser drawer, and it glides silently. Inside is a pair of lacy panties that caught my eye earlier today. Soft, pale pink, the way I imagine her pussy would look.

I close my eyes, lifting the crotch to my nose, taking deep breaths, and letting the aroma of her pussy carry me away. Even clean, they hold her scent. It makes my heart thud almost painfully against my ribs, and my cock stirs to life in an instant until there's nothing for me to do but free myself and wrap my fist around my straining, swollen length.

I open my eyes and watch her sleep, fisting my cock, imagining the satisfaction of crawling on top of her and stripping her naked, running my tongue along every inch of her smooth, supple body. I can almost hear her frantic, dirty whispers. *Just like that. More. Harder. You're going to make me come.*

She's going to make me come. I stare at those pointy nipples, entranced by the way every breath leaves them close to showing themselves, teasing me, even when she's asleep. I'll make her pay for that too. I'll make her pay for all of it.

A familiar tingle builds at the base of my spine, and my balls feel heavy, swollen, and ready for release. Faster, faster, my fist is a blur, my strangled breaths coming quicker until I wrap the garment around my throbbing head a second before release sends my seed spilling onto the cotton and lace. Satisfaction overtakes me before the final spurt soaks into the fabric, and I smile to myself as I tuck my already soft dick into my pants. What to do with the soiled panties? Balling them up, I shove them in my pocket as a souvenir, wondering if she'll miss them.

I know when enough is enough, and I've already done plenty tonight. Before I go, I take one last look at her, memorizing the perfect profile, the look of peace and contentment now on her face. *Enjoy it while you can, Emilia.* I leave the top drawer of her dresser open an inch as a calling card, something for her to find when she wakes up, asking herself whether she's imagining things.

I almost hate to leave, but it's a good thing I choose to go when I do because my phone rings before I reach the curb in front of the building. No way would I have escaped unnoticed if that happened in the apartment.

Fucking Dante.

"I told you, I have shit I'm taking care of right now," I mutter as I cross the street on the way back to the car. "Will you ever learn to leave enough alone?"

"Is my favorite thirty-year-old toddler done throwing a tantrum, or do you need a little more time?" he asks with a weary sigh. "Let me know, and I'll wait," he taunts, and I have to roll my shoulders, fighting the building tension.

Not even Papa can do that to me—talk down at me and try to make me feel small. Because my father wouldn't. He knows better. My older brother, on the other hand? Every day, he decides to test me.

"What's the problem? It had better be good after you've hounded me all night," I warn, checking the car's interior and glancing underneath before getting inside. A man can't be too careful.

"We have a problem," he states as if I'm unaware of what has been going on.

"And up until now, things were going so well." My sarcasm can't be helped.

He ignores me. "There were Vitali spies at the club Friday night."

My heart stops for a brief, shocked moment. "And we know this how?"

"From one of our paid guys down at the precinct. He got word of it while he was out in a Vitali bar earlier tonight. Frankie was a bigger problem than we guessed."

"I don't wanna hear his name," I bite out.

"I wish I could help you with that. I really do."

I'm starting to get a headache. "How was *he* a bigger problem?"

"He told you he was in over his head with gambling debt?" he asks. "That they offered to clear it for him?"

"That was his story," I growl out, remembering how he blubbered and begged.

"It's starting to look like that's all it was. A story. And as soon as they got word he got picked up and taken to the club for questioning, they were there too. Waiting to see what would happen."

I stare out the windshield, still parked, unsure I trust

myself to drive when I can barely see straight for the fresh rage blazing its way through my system. In the end, he couldn't be honest with me. It wouldn't have changed anything. He would've died anyway. He could've at least died like a man with a clear conscience.

"And apparently, there's been word of you flirting with some girl who ended up going into your office later on. Is this true?"

Motherfucker. How the fuck did anybody see that? "It was after. I took care of it."

He grunts. "But here's the thing. They think she saw something, and I'm not sure they're wrong."

An icy finger traces its way down my spine. "What are you saying?" I ask.

"I'm saying if they don't get their hands on her first, we're going to have to. We can't afford loose ends, and she sounds like one."

"I'm telling you, she didn't see a fucking thing." I should slice Vinny's balls off for being a clumsy, stupid asshole.

"Do me a favor and explain that to the Vitali for me, would you? Because I've got a lot of other things on my hands." He ends the call before I can tell him to shove his imperious attitude up his ass.

She's not a Vitali spy. That much I know for sure. It's instinct. No way would she get in bed with them, not Little Miss Goody Two Shoes up there. There's still a fucking stuffed bear on her bed, for God's sake.

But they're going to find her. They already may have. And that's a problem.

When they decide to pay a visit, they're not going to stop at jerking off into her panties and moving things around so she'll think she's either going crazy or being stalked.

The only question left is what to do about it. Do I step back and let them kill her, thus doing me a favor in the long run by eliminating a witness? Keeping my hands clean?

Or do I watch her back since I'm the man who deserves to claim her punishment for myself?

7

EMILIA

"**W**hat a fucking mess."

If Craig has one skill, it's his ability to sum up a situation in a handful of words. I can't disagree as we stand side by side, watching the forensics investigators work the scene of yet another vicious killing. This time, a trio of young men were shot execution-style and left face down in an empty lot between two currently unused commercial buildings. The killer or killers pulled the victims' driver's licenses from their wallets and left them on the corresponding men's backs as if they were doing us a favor, saving us a step.

It took all of five minutes to pull their extensive records. "No surprise, them working for the Santoros," I murmur, gazing around at the surrounding area and noting the brisk foot traffic on this block. Something tells me nobody heard anything, though. Witnesses tend to feel safer that way, especially when a murder bears all the hallmarks of a gangland execution. "I'm starting to wish I never heard the name," I mumble under my breath.

Captain Stuart joins us, hunching his shoulders against

the unseasonably cold air. The sky is slate gray, and the clouds seem to hang low enough that even somebody as short as me could reach up and swirl them around. "Our intel sources are all coming back with the same information. It's all tied up in a shipment of guns out of Sicily picked up by ATF."

"Sicily. That's the Santoros, right?" Craig asks.

"And Allesandro Vitali wants to make sure everybody knows he tipped them off." The captain sighs while rubbing a hand over his scruff-covered jaw. "I'd bet my pension on him plotting to knock his old man off and speed up the process of taking over the family business. He's chomping at the bit already."

Allesandro has a notoriously short temper as it is, and according to the research I've poured so much of my time into, he might be the worst possible person to be in charge of a wealthy, violent mafia family. Only Giorgio has ever held his son in check. With nobody holding the reins, things are bound to get bloodier.

"You okay, Washington?" Craig drapes an arm over my shoulders before I can stop him. "You're shivering."

"I'm fine. It's cold out, but it won't kill me." I shrug him off as I always do when he finds a reason to initiate physical contact. I wonder if he'd be so chivalrous toward his wife if she shivered. Part of me wants to ask.

Instead of starting a fight in front of our captain, I jerk my chin toward the coffee shop at the end of the block. "I'll get something to warm me up. Be right back." I'm already on my way across the street before I realize I never offered to pick anything up for them. I'd turn back, but it feels safer to put space between my partner and me when I want to claw his eyes out for touching and infantilizing me and somehow sexually harassing me at the same time.

I'm on edge. That much is clear.

Days later, the sensation is stronger than ever. I can't shake the feeling I'm being watched. Somebody *is* following me. Invading my space. The energy in my apartment is all off and out of whack. There's a charge in the air when I get home at night. I've considered getting a hotel room for the sake of a night's peace.

A shriek pierces the air, and I jump, then curse myself when two kids run past. I can't handle being in public now? What the hell is happening to me?

"Don't push yourself too hard, sweetie." How many times have I heard that one from my parents? You'd think they'd be proud of me, but all they seem interested in is whether I'm pushing myself too hard. Who wants to hear that day in and day out?

I'm almost relieved this situation coincides with their three-month trip through the Australian Outback since one look at the circles under my eyes would set off an explosion of questions and concerns.

I wonder whether they have a point. Am I working myself too hard? My nerves are shredded, and I can't sleep. I'd swear there was somebody in my room a few nights back. At the time, I thought I was having weird dreams thanks to the wine, but waking up to a partly open dresser drawer was like a bucket of ice water being poured over my head.

I'm starting to doubt what's real and what's my imagination.

I order a large coffee without thinking much about it. I'm too busy examining the small but bustling shop and its customers. Is the guy in the corner looking at me over the top of his newspaper? Is the woman typing on her laptop watching me before I look her way? It seems as if her head snapped around, and her typing picked up speed.

The walls are closing in. My heart is going to pound

out of my chest. I need air. There are too many people around. The second my coffee is poured, I'm on my way to the door, almost fleeing until I burst out into the cold again and pull in as deep a breath as I can manage. Something has to give. I can't take this much longer.

I have to get myself together before facing Craig or the captain again. Coffee was probably not the best idea. Lord knows I don't need to be any jumpier, but then I could use the caffeine to shake off the brain fog three nights of broken sleep have left me with.

I'm making up things in my head. I saw something horrible—or think I did—and it screwed with my brain. Should I talk to the department therapist? It would mean admitting the risk I took that night.

The light in front of me turns green, and I should cross and get back to work down the block. Knowing Craig would never let me live it down if I cracked up and needed to go on leave is what propels me off the curb, ready to throw my shoulders back and push my way through whatever the hell is eating at me.

"Emilia!"

I freeze at the sound of a man barking my name, then turn on my heel and look in the direction the sound came from. It was loud and sharp enough that it sounded like a warning.

"Look out!" a woman screams, and it rings out a split second before a speeding car clips my right hip and thigh. My coffee goes flying, and so do I, hitting the ground while sudden, sharp pain makes the world tilt on its side and spin around me. My cry of surprise is drowned out by a revving engine and squealing tires, soon followed by the concerned voices of witnesses now flying to my side.

Where is he? I didn't see him, whoever he was. He called my name and stopped me from getting run over.

"I'M TELLING YOU, I'm fine," I huff out, frustration seeping into my words.

The look the men exchange makes me want to scream. I know exactly what they're thinking. I guess I would think it if I was in their shoes. I mean, I am lying on a gurney in the ER after being x-rayed.

"You're going to take a week off, the way the doctor advised." The captain narrows his eyes when I try to fight. "I'm not listening to any of your arguments. You were hit by a car, Emilia."

"Sideswiped," I remind him.

"Sideswiped hard enough for a doctor to tell you to stay on the couch for a week," Craig reminds me, and I seriously wish he hadn't been around to overhear my conversation with the doctor. The way he folds his arms and stares down at me, I wonder if he's mistaking me for one of his kids.

"You have plenty of PTO banked, and it's there to be used." The captain zips his jacket. "I'll drive you home, and we'll arrange to have your car driven home for you from the station. You have nothing to worry about."

So he thinks.

So I wish I could believe it.

Before Craig steps out so I can take off this thin hospital gown and get dressed, I ask, "How did you know what happened?"

"What do you mean?"

"Did you shout my name? Right before the car hit me?" I question, needing to know who called out to me.

He tips his head to the side, and I can practically hear him asking himself if I need a psych evaluation. "No. We heard a woman scream and looked over, and you were already on the ground."

Right, and the voice wasn't coming from his direction, anyway. "Somebody shouted my name. I'm sure of it," I share, hoping they can get a lead.

"Maybe somebody who recognized you?"

If they had, why didn't they come running like everybody else who witnessed the accident? If that's, in fact, what it was.

His narrowed eyes tell me I'm in for an interrogation. "Are you really okay? You seem very shaken."

"Like you said, I was hit by a car today." I wave him out of the curtained-off area so I can slowly, painfully get dressed.

All right, I can admit there would be no way for me to work feeling the way I do. An ugly, deep purple bruise runs from my hip down to the middle of my thigh. My knees are bruised and scraped up as well as the palms of my hands. All in all, I got lucky, even if I don't feel that way now, when every nerve ending throbs painfully.

Did somebody see the car coming and try to warn me? Who would do that? How could they possibly know who I am?

The question is still fresh in my mind by the time I get home. No way am I leaving this apartment in the immediate future. It took both Craig and the captain supporting me on either side to get me up the three floors. Now that the rush of adrenaline has dwindled, the pain is fresher, more raw, bringing it to the forefront.

Thankfully, they did send me home with a small bottle of painkillers. I would avoid them, but I don't think I have that luxury at the moment.

After running a hot bath, I take one of the pills and wash it down with a lot of water, then get undressed. I'm hoping the combination of meds and soaking in a hot bath will lessen the soreness. If only I felt safe in my home. Knowing I couldn't possibly move fast enough to defend myself if danger came knocking is torture, plain and simple. Rather than leave my gun in its holster, I place it on top of the toilet tank, which should be close enough to reach it if anything happens.

After what feels like forever, I lower myself into the steaming water, then settle back with my neck against a rolled-up towel.

Of all the stupid things that could possibly happen.

I don't want to believe someone saw me crossing the street and hit the gas, but…

I sink a little deeper in the water, shutting out the rest of that thought before it can fully form. I am not going to let myself go down that path. Nobody is trying to kill me.

But who called my name?

The click of a lock disengaging doesn't get my heart thumping right away. I'm floating in a haze, grateful for the pain to ease for a little while. But it's enough that it stirs me, making me alert, and I hold my breath to listen hard in case I once again have imagined something that didn't happen.

But it did happen because the hinges on the front door squeak ever so slightly as someone eases it open.

Fuck. I reach out, straining for the gun, which now feels so far away. The pill! I'm looking at the room through a fisheye lens, everything distorted and a little dreamy. I may as well have left the gun in the holster by the front door. It feels so far away. My heart is pounding, and I'm gasping for air, rising up on my knees, leaning over the edge of the tub, and straining for the gun.

Tap. Tap. Tap. Footsteps cross my living room, coming closer to the open bathroom door.

There's no way I can be quiet. They probably know I'm here anyway, whoever they are. I half climb, half fall out of the tub after trying one more time to reach the gun and knocking it to the floor. Luckily, I left the safety engaged as it skitters between the toilet and the vanity without accidentally discharging. I slide my shivering body over the cold tile, reaching out in desperation, fumbling to grasp my only chance of survival.

The footsteps stop, and I look up from the puddle I've made on the floor into the eyes of a cold-blooded killer. He doesn't have to say a word. He only has to stare down at me with dark, dead eyes for me to know exactly why he's here. What he came for.

This is it. This is where I die. Wet and naked on a cold tile floor.

He raises his gun, aiming for my head.

A burst of something warm, red, and sticky splashes the wall, floor, and open door. It lands on me too. I can't process either the ear-splitting sound that preceded the splash or the splash itself, looking down at the blood now running over my arms and chest.

It's not my blood.

The man's body hits the floor like a ton of bricks.

It's then I see the man behind him who blew his brains all over my bathroom.

Luca Santoro.

His face is a hardened mask of fury and hatred, and I recognize it as the same expression he wore in his office when I walked in on what he did to the bloody, broken man in the chair.

He steps over the corpse, and nothing matters more than getting away from this monster because he might have saved my life, but he might also want to take it himself. I slide away and throw an arm over my face, unable to stop from cringing and shaking.

His hand closes around my forearm, and I fight to pull away, but he doesn't twist. He doesn't squeeze, break, or explain what brought him here in the first place. He simply lifts me to my feet.

"That settles it," he grunts out. "You're coming with me."

8

LUCA

"I don't understand." She's shivering, naked, wet with water from her bath and the blood of the son of a bitch whose useless life I ended. "What are you saying? What do you mean?" she questions, one right after another.

"You're in shock." And I have a problem on my hands, one big enough that even the sight of a wet, naked body like the one in front of me doesn't register. There's no going back now. I've staked my claim. There's a dead assassin at my feet and a growing pool of blood painting the tiled floor. We don't have time for her to break down.

But that's what she's determined to do. Her teeth are chattering, and her eyes bulge until they're too big for her face. I doubt she realizes she's completely exposed to my gaze. She's so overwhelmed by the past few moments. "I... am not going anywhere with you." Her weak attempt at freeing herself from my grip is laughable. My fingers only dig into the soft flesh of her upper arm until she sucks in a pained wince.

"Here's what you're going to do if you plan on living to

see tomorrow," I whisper, hauling her in close until I can smell her fear. "You are going to drain the water from the tub. You're going to get in the tub, and you are going to turn on the shower, and you're going to wash yourself off. Got it? Or do I have to do it for you?"

That's what shakes her out of it. The idea of me bathing her was all it took to make her upper lip curl in a disgusted sneer and to cover her tits with her free arm. "Hell, no. I'll do it."

One look at the colorful span of skin on her right leg makes me think otherwise. "You're sure you can handle it?" I ask, raising a brow.

"Yes." Her gaze hardens, her eyes narrowing. "I can do it."

"Good. Make it fast." I release her, noting where her gaze immediately falls, the semi-automatic on the floor beside the toilet. "I'll pick this up for you," I offer, taking it and leaving her groaning softly as if she was planning on using the damn thing on me.

Too predictable.

Then I leave her to it, heading to her bedroom and grabbing a cheap tote bag from the top shelf of her closet. I move quickly, pulling clothes from her drawers and shoving them inside the bag. Once the shock wears off, she'll wonder how I knew where to find everything. That's a situation I can address later once I have us out of danger. Because whether I want to admit it or not, I've inserted myself into the situation and chosen my side.

What the hell am I thinking? I've been accused of going rogue in the past, following my own rules, essentially telling naysayers to fuck off if they have a problem with my decision-making. But this is a lot even for me.

What was the alternative? Letting one of Vitali's thugs run her down today, allowing one of them to murder her in cold blood? If anybody is going to do that, it will be me. He will not have the satisfaction of claiming her life.

And unlike him, I prefer to do these sorts of things myself. I don't send thugs after a wounded woman. Only some fucking coward would do that. If I'm lodging a bullet between her eyes, I'm looking into those eyes while I do it.

"Luca?" Her voice is shaky when she calls me from the bathroom after she's finished and the water is off. "There's too much blood. I can't step over it."

I reach into the linen closet between the bedroom and bathroom and pull out a handful of towels, which I then drop on the floor. Like magic, they go from white to red. A second layer helps conceal the blood pooling on the white and black checkered tile.

When I reach out to help her, she pointedly ignores my outstretched hand, stepping carefully onto the towels rather than dipping her bare feet into the blood of the man who was moments away from ending her life before I caught up to him.

"How did you know?" she asks once she's out of the room and doesn't have to look at the corpse anymore.

"It doesn't matter. I need to get you out of here before I send somebody to clean the place up."

"No. I want to know now." She sways unsteadily, and instinct makes me reach for her before she jerks away. "Tell me. How did you know somebody came up here to shoot me?"

"Stop with the fucking questions." I snarl, holding her gaze until she looks away. "Does it matter? You're alive now, thanks to me."

"I'm not leaving this apartment until you tell me the truth. What's it going to be?" She folds her arms over her towel-covered chest. In all this excitement, I haven't bothered admiring her body, but this is all it takes to get my cock to behave? The thought of what will happen if the Vitalis find out what went down before I get her out of here?

And to think, I was going to toy with her some more. I should shoot that bastard again for destroying my plans and speeding up the timeline. Some things can't be helped. After drawing a deep breath, I drop the bombshell. "I've been watching you, *Detective Washington.*"

Her eyes go round, her lips pulling back from her teeth in a grimace before she recovers. "I don't know what you're talking about?"

White heat slashes through my veins at her lies. "You know damn well what I'm fucking talking about." Taking her towel in my fist, I pull her close, looming over her shivering form. "And unless you want another four or five assholes coming up here to blow you away, you're going to drop the attitude and do as I say. *Now.*"

All she does is dig her heels in, baring her teeth in a snarl. "I'm not going anywhere with you! You must be out of your goddamn mind."

"Am I?" I ask, arching a brow. She gasps sharply when I yank the towel from her body, then again when I take a handful of her dripping hair and tilt her head back so we're looking into each other's eyes. "You walked into my club and tried to flirt your way into busting up my business. Which of us has lost our mind, *Detective?* Either you come with me, or you live the rest of your short life wishing you had. Because I'm not always going to be around to save your cute little ass the way I did this morning."

A soft sigh eases its way from between her parted lips. "It was you. You stopped me."

I nod, watching understanding dawn on her and soften her features. "Now. Put on some clothes before I change my mind and decide to keep you naked. I'm taking you somewhere safe."

"But why?" she whispers. "Why would you do this? You know who I am, you know what—"

Cupping her jaw in my free hand, I press my fingers against her soft flesh until she grunts. "Because you and I have unfinished business, that's why. And nobody is going to kill you before the score is settled."

She shakes my hand away with a sudden snap of her head, her lip curling in disgust. "Fuck off. If you're only going to kill me anyway—"

"I will kill you here and now if you don't stop with the fucking questions unless you would rather I throw you over my shoulder and carry you naked out into the cold." I let my gaze drift south, taking in her shivering body. "Maybe I'll do that anyway. Give the neighbors a nice show. People need to see this."

"You are a vile, disgusting pig."

"Nice language, considering it could be *your* brains splattered on the walls and not some piece of shit assassin's." She sucks in a sharp breath, and I know I've gotten through to her for now. "Dress yourself. I won't repeat myself again."

I step into the hall and dial Vinny, who answers on the first ring. "Where have you been? We were—"

I cut him off with a grunt. "I need you at this address." I rattle it off for him while staring at the corpse I created. "I have some garbage that needs to be taken out. This is between you and me *only*. Understood?"

"You got it." That's all it takes, and I know he's on his way. He can redeem himself for his unforgivable fuck-up last Friday night.

I hear her in there, getting her shit together. The only reason I feel confident leaving her alone is my familiarity with her bedroom. "Let's fucking go!" I bark out, and a soft whimper is her only reply, so I look into the room to find her sitting at the foot of the bed, running a hand under her nose, gesturing to the sneakers on the floor.

She's managed to pull on a thick sweater and leggings, but that's as far as she's gotten. "I can't bend down to put them on," she sniffles, wet hair hanging in front of her face. "I took a pain pill before I got in the bath. I'm all clumsy."

Fuck me. "Stop crying, for fuck's sake," I say sharply, my voice filled with exasperation. Bending down, I fix the socks she barely managed to get on her feet before jamming them into her shoes.

I've barely finished when there's sudden pressure against my temple. Something small, hard. "You never found the one I keep under my mattress, asshole." She snarls.

This duplicitous bitch—yet at the same time, my dick twitches like it's sensed something of interest. "What do you think you're going to do?" I question, staying completely still while she presses the muzzle to my skull. "You're going to kill me? What happens when the next guy comes for you? And the one after that?"

Slowly, I raise my head, meeting a steely gaze that doesn't soften under my stare. What a shame we're natural enemies since this is a woman I could have fun with. "Because this doesn't end with my murder, Detective," I whisper, savoring her sharp breaths that quicken as I raise myself between her parted thighs. "In fact, you kill me now, and you may as well kiss your life goodbye. They will never stop coming for you."

"Bullshit," she hisses out.

I lean into the gun, then smile. "Come on, then. Go for it. Kill me and see whether it's all bullshit."

"Why?" she demands through clenched teeth, pressing the gun harder. "Tell me why."

The gun doesn't waver as I lean closer, daring her to pull the trigger when I know she won't. Not when she's so busy staring at my mouth the way I can't help but stare at hers, remembering the feel of those lips against mine. "Because the Vitali family thinks you are a spy for us, and my family thinks you're a spy for them."

She gives her head the tiniest shake. "But you know that's not true."

"Because I know you're a fucking detective, and do you think you would be breathing at this moment if I told my father that? You would already be in the morgue. You owe me your life, Detective Washington." I chuckle darkly. "You owe me a great many things, and I intend to collect."

"I don't owe you anything," she snaps, but her voice has lost its edge. She's weakening, and I know why. It's the reason I'm on the edge myself, almost burning from the desire to kiss her again. She's fighting it and losing, almost forgetting the gun she's no longer pressing so hard against my skull.

"I've kept you alive," I remind her before lunging forward, ready to taste her again.

Her head snaps back before I can make contact, eyes narrowed into slits. "And that's your excuse for stalking me?" she grits out. "Breaking into my apartment, fucking with me all week?"

For a woman on drugs, she's surprisingly sharp. "Something like that."

All at once, I grab her wrist and press two fingers against the heel of her hand hard enough to loosen her grip and take the weapon from her. "Narcotics fuck with your reflexes," I inform her before tucking the Glock 9mm into my waistband along with her service weapon.

"Why don't you leave me here?" There's no bravado in her voice anymore. It's pure resignation. Fatigue. "If you're going to kill me anyway, do it and get it over with. I would rather die than go anywhere with you."

And the thing is, when our eyes meet, I see the truth in those blue depths. She means it. She would rather die than leave this apartment with me. All that realization does is stir the resentment and bitterness I've battled all week to new life.

I savor her gasp of pain when I pull her to her feet. "You don't get to decide how this ends. You're going to learn what happens to people who think they can take what's mine." With that, I gather the straps of her tote bag and sling it over my shoulder, then pull her by her wrist from the bedroom into the living room. "Put your coat on. Make it fast. We don't have much time."

"Where are you taking me?"

"It's not your business."

She punches her fists through her sleeves. "No, of course. It's not my business where I'm going with you."

"You can come with me, or you can go to the morgue, Detective... one or the other. It's your choice," I offer with a perturbed shrug.

"Some choice," she snarls. "Why not ask how much shit I want to be piled on my shit sandwich?"

If anything, I prefer her this way. She's no longer pulling the innocent act the way she did back at the club. This is the real Emilia, thorns and all. *A thorn in my fucking side.* I need to remember that when she's blazing and snarling and somehow turning me on.

"You're wasting time," I remind her. "Believe me. It would be in your best interest to pick things up."

"You're never going to get away with it." She stands with her back to the door, feet planted as if she's going to bar the way. "You know that, right? You have to know. My captain and my partner dropped me off here earlier. What are they going to think when I've suddenly disappeared? They're going to search for you."

"Let them," I scoff. "Besides. That's my problem, not yours."

"You know, I heard you were a real arrogant son of a bitch. I thought you were intelligent, at least."

I've had about enough of this. She barely stifles a gasp when I shove her back against the closed door, caging her in place with an arm on either side of her body. A squirming, struggling body now dangerously close to mine, so close to making me forget the stakes in favor of playing with what I've only admired and jerked off to so far.

"Now you listen to me." I lean in close, my mouth inches from hers, and savor the panicked little breaths that fan across my face when she struggles for air. "I saved your life twice today. It would have been much easier for me to let Vitali kill you, but here I am. As far as I'm concerned, your life belongs to me now, and it would be nice if you showed a little gratitude."

She tosses her head, glaring at me, but I know better. I feel the way she trembles. I hear the tremor in her voice when she asks, "You want me to thank you for destroying my life?"

"Oh, Detective." Her brow creases as if she's pained, telling me she hates when I call her that. "You did that to yourself when you stepped foot in my club. You could have gotten away with it if you hadn't been stupid enough to enter my office. It's fairly clear you don't value your life much as it is. So, don't give me shit now for saving you for myself. And don't pretend you have any say over what happens now or what I plan to do to you. We both know better."

Let her fight it all she wants. She is gripped by terror, the tantalizing aroma oozing from her pores. It does things to me it shouldn't, making my pulse pick up and my cock twitch again in anticipation. "Like it or not, you owe me a debt, and I'm going to see you pay it. And how you do so is my business."

Her eyes dart over my face. "What does that mean?"

"You'll see when the time comes. First things first. Getting you out of here alive before Vitali realizes what happened. Now, are you walking out with me, or am I carrying you with a gag stuffed in your mouth?"

Her eyes narrow, and her nostrils flare. The hate is rolling off her. I'm disappointed but not surprised to find it only makes me want her more. "You're making a big mistake," she warns, and her breathing turns erratic when I draw one of her guns from my waistband and drag it over her tits, almost caressing her, before I lean in to brush my lips against her ear.

As tantalizing as it was to watch her while she slept, knowing she couldn't stop me, this is better. Witnessing fear overtake her no matter how she struggles to hide it. I see her bravado for what it is. A thin veneer meant to conceal her helplessness.

My helpless little Emilia.

"Tell me something I don't know," I whisper before savoring her soft, defeated groan.

9

EMILIA

I need to think.

My brain is foggy, and my reflexes are slow. I'm sitting in a car with a man I hate to the very depths of my soul. A man who has spent the past week toying with me, breaking into my home, and screwing with my head until I was on the verge of breaking down. A man with a gun in his lap, which he's already used to get me moving down the stairs and out the door.

A man who kept me from being run over today.

A man who killed to prevent my death.

A man whose kiss has never been far from the forefront of my thoughts since the moment our lips met, and he set my body on fire.

What the hell is going on here?

His anger is thick enough to steal the air from inside the car as we pull away from the curb across the street from my building. All this time, he knew exactly where to find me. He could've killed me at any point. He didn't. But I'll be damned if I give him a gold star. This is not someone I can trust. A tiger could be raised in captivity and treated as a house cat, but that won't make it gentle when its instincts kick in and it remembers it's a predator.

And that's who this man is. Someone who could shoot a stranger dead without flinching, like it was just another day at the office for him. That's what happens when you don't have a soul.

He has to know he may as well have signed his own death warrant when he pulled me from that apartment at gunpoint. There is no way there won't be search parties formed once word spreads that I'm missing. With all his faults, Craig is still a solid detective. He's bound to find something in that apartment that ties Luca to my disappearance.

Or am I only telling myself that?

Dammit, I need to think, but it's like trying to wade through semi-set Jell-O. My thoughts are plodding. The panic that's flooded my body and kicked off my fight-or-flight response isn't helping them move any faster.

He took my gun.

Remembering the way his firm, tight body pinned me to the apartment door leaves me doubting I could beat him in hand-to-hand combat, especially when my hip and leg hurt like hell after nearly running down three flights of stairs without anyone's help. I didn't bring the pills with me, either.

I'm going to have to tough it out. That's for the best, anyway. I can't afford to be foggy around him after this. I need to stay sharp.

What do I know about him? I close my eyes, thinking back on what I've already learned. He's the second son after Dante. He has a younger sister named Guilia. The family still lives together in the Santoro compound out on Long Island, with Dante and Luca staying in small cottages away from the main house. I've studied drone footage and looked over Google Earth images of the entire property.

What good is any of that going to do me now?

Luca was first arrested when he was seventeen for a shooting during a fight at a bar he was much too young to visit, but of course, the family lawyer managed to get the charges dropped. He sailed through the open doors of his jail cell that very day and never so much as stood before a judge. He's been connected to countless disappearances between then and the time when his father placed him in charge of the club, which serves as the family's last connection to legitimacy and likely serves as a money laundering front in the meantime.

He's always gotten away with it. That's what money can buy—a lack of consequences. This man has never dealt with repercussions in his life.

I guess now is as good a time as any to introduce him to the concept. All I need is the courage to stand up and fight, but right now, my courage might as well be up on the moon. Panic and dread are the dominant forces pumping blood through my veins hard enough that the sound drums in my ears.

"Are you taking me to your house?" I ask as the world moves by in a blur. I'd push out the door if he weren't controlling the locks from his door. Jumping from a moving vehicle doesn't sound like a good time, but I'm as good as dead if I stay with him.

He blurts out a laugh. "Right. I'm sure everyone in my family would be thrilled to meet you."

Because they're such a great group of lovely people. My tongue hurts from all the biting I'm putting it through. "All you have to do is tell them I'm not a spy."

"Again, *Detective*." God, I hate the way he says that like it's a bad word, something to be ashamed of. "The only way I could remotely prove you have nothing to do with the Vitali is to announce your job title. That would not do you any favors. Even then, you could be on the take. Though if any of them took a look at that apartment of yours, they'd soon change their minds."

"You must not have much influence in your family, then, if you can't convince them," I taunt.

"Nice try." He gives me a filthy look before snickering and turning his gaze toward the road. "You're wasting your time trying to get into my head."

Dammit. I pushed too hard. "I wasn't trying to—"

"Enough bullshit," he snarls out, cutting me off, and the way he swings from cold to hot and back again chills me. "We're not playing cops and robbers here. You're dealing with people who would murder you, then go home and kiss their wife and kids before sitting down to dinner. It means nothing. They're protecting what's theirs, or don't you understand that? You should, considering you've made it your business to meddle in ours."

"I know all about your bullshit macho excuse for loyalty," I fire back. "The so-called code you live by."

"You don't know the first thing. You're still speaking in clichés, acting like the shit you've seen in the media is true. Let me clue you in. Consider it a free lesson. The sons of bitches have no honor. Alessandro Vitali? All he sees is what his, or what he thinks is his. You tried to get in the way of that. Therefore, you are the enemy. And you must die."

"But I didn't try to get in the way of it," I argue, not understanding.

"Oh, right." He laughs. "I'm sure the Vitali name had nothing to do with any of this. You have a hard-on for the name Santoro, and that's it. Stop wasting your breath before I pull into the next parking lot and put that mouth to better use."

I turn my face away, staring out the window rather than asking what use he's referring to. To think, the night we met, I was so taken with him I might have gone ahead and let him use me the way he just hinted. As it is, there's a telltale warmth between my thighs at the idea. Good thing he can't tell, or I'd die of shame.

"Remember," he mutters. "They think you were at the club that night to get intel on the business I was conducting before you were arrogant enough to get in the way. Don't think about blaming me for that, either. You brought this on yourself, trying to be a hero, trying to single-handedly accomplish what hundreds of cops, detectives, Feds, lawyers, and more have failed at for years."

I shiver at his words. The worst part is he's not saying this to frighten me. He means it. I hear it in his flat, no-nonsense delivery.

"And what about your family?" I counter. "They won't listen to reason?"

A growl rumbles in his chest, loud enough for me to hear. "Let me worry about my family. Don't talk about things you don't have the first idea of," he warns, but it only spurs me on.

"I hit a sore spot, didn't I?" I venture since, no matter how terrifying he is, part of me wants to push his buttons.

"Shut your fucking mouth," he snaps before stepping down on the gas pedal and making the car leap forward, weaving back and forth between the cars around us until I have to close my eyes to keep myself from screaming.

This man won't be satisfied until he's broken my mind completely.

Don't let him. Don't give in.

I have no plans to, but then I didn't plan to be

kidnapped today, either. I sure as hell didn't plan on negotiating for my life or wondering which breath would be my last. But I'm not going to whimper and cower, especially when I know how it turns him on when I do.

I felt the erection that began to stir when he had me up against the door. The way it twitched when he ran the muzzle of my own gun over my breasts, tracing my curves with steel instead of his fingers.

And only I know how repulsed I was by my reaction to it and shuddered not only in fear but in need. The memory stirs heat to life in my core, which sparks the heat of humiliation in my cheeks. It has to be the drugs in my system screwing with my head.

Is he only trying to protect me by dragging me from my home? Or is he saving me for something worse, something so awful it would make me wish he'd been a second later in pulling the trigger that saved my life? I can't imagine a scenario where keeping me alive would be in his best interest, yet that seems to be his MO. He said he wants to be the one to settle the score. Why not kill me in the apartment, then?

I can barely keep my head up by the time we cross North Jersey and enter Pennsylvania. As hard as I try, there's no stifling a yawn. I've hardly slept in days, I'm drugged, and the strain I have put on my adrenal glands today has me struggling to keep my eyes open.

He found that I was a detective while I was unconscious, at his mercy. *How much worse can he do now if I fall asleep and let down my guard?*

When I yawn again, he clicks his tongue in ridicule. "Go the fuck to sleep already," he mutters. "Do you think I'll slit that smooth throat of yours? Or maybe paint the inside of my Mercedes with your brains like I painted your bathroom? After all the trouble I went through today? For fuck's sake."

The memory of splattered blood running down my skin stirs nausea in my gut. "Pardon me if I don't trust the homicidal maniac stalker who practically shoved me into a car at gunpoint."

"Don't exaggerate." He sneers. "You're the one who put a gun to my head, remember? And don't think I'm going to forgive that. As far as I'm concerned, it goes on your tab."

I'd ask what that's supposed to mean, but I'm not sure I want to know. I settle for muttering, "I hope this makes you feel very big and important, talking to me that way."

"I hope you know my ego isn't so fragile that I would respond to your pitiful attempt at insulting it." He slides a disparaging smirk my way. "You're boring me. Take a nap. Get your head together."

That's the first reasonable thing he's said so far. I need to get my head together. No, chipping at his ego isn't going to be what saves my life and keeps me in one piece, unharmed by him.

But he has his weaknesses. He's already revealed more than one, with me being the common denominator. My fear. His control over me. He gets off on it the way he got off on infiltrating my life. If I'm going to survive, I need to use his weakness against him, which means playing up my fear. That won't take much acting skill. I'll never forget how empty his eyes looked when they met mine moments after he committed murder.

How he felt... nothing.

"I think I will close my eyes," I murmur, groaning as I shift my weight in the seat. "I should have laid down across the back, come to think of it. I'm in a lot of pain."

"It won't hurt when you're asleep."

"Thank you very much, Dr. Death." I allow my eyes to drift shut while he laughs humorlessly, and we speed down the interstate to a destination unknown to me.

As my thoughts drift, the beginnings of a plan percolate in the back of my mind—use his desire against him until he's too twisted up to see straight and can't bear the thought of going through with his murderous plans. It's everything I've avoided doing since I joined the academy— using my body to get ahead—despite what others claim about it being the only path for someone my age to reach my current position.

But now, it's my only option. Now, I don't feel quite so powerless.

All I need now is to give my body the memo before the inexplicable heat he stirs to life ends up burning me.

10

LUCA

It's not very late when we reach the safe house, but the sky is gray enough today to leave darkness surrounding us when I pull up behind the simple, single-story cabin hidden in the deep woods on the outskirts of the Poconos. The air out here is clear and clean. If it weren't for the clouds hanging low and thick in the sky, there would be plenty of stars to admire.

Not that I have time for that, anyway. "Hey." I nudge my sleeping companion, who only mumbles before turning her head away. "Wake up. We're here." I nudge her again when she doesn't move and wonder if she's in the grips of a dream.

"Where are we?" Her voice is thick with sleep, scratchy as she sits bolt upright like she only now remembered everything that came before this.

"We're someplace safe where nobody from the Vitali crew will find you."

"You brought me out to the middle of nowhere?" she questions, turning around in all directions as she takes in where we are, her head snapping back and forth.

"Something like that." In reality, another ten-minute drive, we could visit one of the many resorts dotting the landscape, but she doesn't need to know that. The less she knows, the better.

For both of us.

What she needs is help getting out of the car. I should let her struggle on her own, but I'm not a completely heartless bastard. She's been in the car for an hour longer than necessary, thanks to traffic on Route 80, and was already in pain before stiffness settled in, making her more miserable.

Yet when I generously offer to help her out of the car, she flinches away like a skittish animal. "I'm fine," she mumbles, letting her hair hang in front of her face rather than pushing it back as if that would help her hide from me.

If there's one thing I never do, it's begging. "Suit yourself. I'll meet you inside once you realize there's no hope of getting away on foot." Her strangled whimper shouldn't light me up the way it does, but then nothing about how she affects me makes any sense.

By the time she clearly decides it's for the best to join me in the cabin, I have already built a fire in the small hearth. It lights and warms the room, making it almost cozy enough that I could forget why I'm here.

I watch as she takes in her surroundings. The open floor plan makes the small but pleasant living room and the kitchen beyond visible. It's a little rustic, but there's running water, and once I flip on the lights, she can get a better look. "This is nice," she quietly offers.

"Don't feel like you have to flatter me." I lock the door behind her, then look her up and down. "Now. Do I tie you up, or are you going to behave yourself?"

Her wide eyes dart away from mine, arms crossing over her slim middle. "Don't tie me up. Please."

Hmm. Is it this easy to steal her fire and subdue her? I should be glad, but there's nothing but disappointment at the thought of breaking her so effortlessly.

"Bedroom's that way," I continue, pointing to the room in question and watching her squirm. "Bathroom's beside it."

"There's only one bedroom?" Her gaze shifts to where I gestured as she chews on her full lip.

I can't help but be momentarily distracted by the movement, needing to snap myself out of it. "What about it?"

Rather than explain herself, which she doesn't need to do anyway, she looks toward the bathroom. "I need to wash up again. I was sort of in a hurry earlier, and I want to scrub off my top layer of skin." She rubs her arms through her sweater, and now I notice how she leans against the door and only rests the toes of her right foot against the floor.

Let her pretend she's holding it together, but she's in pain.

When I block the doorway to the bathroom and its clawfoot tub, she falls back a step and winces after putting weight on her injured leg. "What?" she whispers.

"I'm wondering if I can trust you." I take my time looking her up and down, arching an eyebrow while dragging out the moment. "You're not going to pull anything stupid, are you?"

"You know I'm unarmed," she mutters, staring at my designer shoes rather than looking me in the eye. "And I can barely walk as it is. Am I going to stage a coup?"

"You might try," I counter, not letting my guard down.

"And I might be ready to claw my skin off because I can still feel that man's blood on me." Her voice cracks, and she lowers her head until her chin touches her chest. "Please. Torment me all you want, but let me do this first. I can't stand it."

Yes, that's right. Give me your weakness. I want to sip it like a fine wine and let it roll on my tongue. The big, brave detective who thought she could single-handedly take me down is reduced to a trembling little girl standing in my shadow.

"Take off your clothes," I murmur while planting my feet and folding my arms.

Her head snaps up, eyes wide. "Wh-what?"

"Strip down. Now. Or else no shower."

"You're joking."

"That's one thing I rarely do," I warn. "And considering the trick you pulled with that little Glock earlier, I'm not about to trust you didn't conceal another weapon somewhere on you." Is that true? Not really. I doubt there's anything else she could have hidden, but then I had no idea there was a gun under her mattress, either.

"I'm not taking my clothes off for you." Defiance tightens her jaw, and yes, I fucking love that, the flash of spirit, and I know there's much more in her. Enough that she thought it was a good idea to pull a gun on me.

Somebody made her this way—all thorns and prickles, wearing an invisible suit of armor that's much too big and heavy for her tiny body to handle. Somebody made her feel as if she was all alone in the big, bad world.

It's not helping her now. "Then let's go to the bedroom, where I'll tie you to the bedframe for lack of trust. This is entirely your fault," I calmly remind her.

All it takes is reaching for her to effectively blow away the last scraps of defiance. She won't look at me as she takes the hem of her sweater in both hands and lifts it over her head. The fire has warmed the room nicely, but she trembles anyway, lowering her gaze while mine rakes over her luscious tits and the tiny, pink nipples tipping them.

"Keep going," I grunt, devouring her with my hungry gaze. I might keep her naked for the hell of it—something to sweeten the shitshow I've brought upon myself. She sniffles and kicks off her sneakers, stumbling awkwardly but maintaining her balance before peeling the leggings away from her body and bending to remove her socks.

Then she stands straight, one hand covering her mound. "Don't you dare," I warn. "As far as I'm concerned, Little Detective, I own you. You do not hide what's mine."

"Just…" She hangs her head again, hair falling in a curtain in front of her face. "Don't hurt me." The soft submission in her voice awakens my dick, and my breath catches when she reveals a neatly shaved mound and the hint of a pink nub peeking from between her lips.

"Turn." I can barely speak, with lust strangling me the way it is. My growing dick springs to life all at once as she slowly turns, granting me a view of her peach of an ass. How I'd love to take a bite.

"Satisfied?" she whispers once we're face-to-face again. Her gaze brushes over my erection and darts away before her face flushes.

"I'm not sure. I might need to do a cavity search." When she flinches, I snicker. "Or maybe not. I suppose I'm satisfied." That's a lie. I am nowhere near satisfied *yet*. But I step aside, anyway, noting how she turns sideways to get past me without making contact. I know there's nothing in the room she could use. Nobody keeps supplies here except for nonperishables in the kitchen cabinets, so there aren't any razor blades or even a nail file she might wield in a misguided moment.

By the time the water begins to run in the tub, my phone starts buzzing. My hackles rise immediately. Fucking Dante. Right on schedule. I slide the phone from my pocket, prepared to tell him to get fucked.

Only it isn't him. It's the extension in Guilia's bedroom. My irritation blows away like petals torn free by the wind. If there's one person who always knows how to set me straight, it's my little sister. That's the talent she was born with.

"Jules, I'm sort of busy," I murmur as gently as I can, with a raging erection owning much of my attention. "Is everything all right?"

There's a long, silent beat before I get a response. "No, son. Everything is not all right."

Realization hits me in the gut like a kick from a horse, and like magic, my erection is history. "Papa. Nice touch, calling from Guilia's room."

"Something told me you might be more inclined to answer if you thought it was your sister calling. I'll pretend I'm not insulted."

Guilt makes the back of my neck prickle. "You know I've never screened my calls when it comes to you," I quietly insist.

"There's a lot of things you've never done before, Luca," he points out in a deceptively smooth voice. "For instance, you've never left town at the drop of a hat without so much as a heads-up to anybody on the crew. You've never become a little more than a ghost around here. I can't tell you how many times I've had to calm your mother down. Three of our men were murdered last night, and you chose now to run off? What are you thinking?"

I can hardly keep up with everything he's thrown at me

all at once. "I'm fine," I assure him, eyeing the open bathroom door. The shower is still running, so there's no way she can hear me. Still, I speak in a low voice, turning my back to the room.

"You're fine? Pardon me if that doesn't ease my mind, son. Especially when I know you ran off with a woman in tow."

Dread wraps itself around my heart, a creeping vine tightening its grip. "What makes you think I have anybody with me?"

"Son. Let's not waste time fucking around," he blows out in frustration.

The full force of the implication is a slap in the face. "You're spying on me?"

"Spying? Is it spying when my son has completely ignored his responsibilities? I was ready to give you space and time after that unfortunate bullshit with our late friend." The briefest mention of Frankie makes my hackles rise. "But now, you're going too far. You haven't worked the club's books in days. You missed sending out orders to replenish the stock down there, and I got a call saying they're running low on just about everything. You've hardly shown your face around here at all. And when you do, you pop in long enough to kiss your mother on the cheek, and then you're gone again." He takes a heavy pause before dropping the hammer. "Tell me the rumors I've heard aren't true."

"It depends on what you've heard," I somehow force through the pinhole my throat has become.

"Don't get smart with me. You know better." His voice is acid, harsh, and corrosive. Anyone who truly knows what my father, the capo, is capable of would relinquish, but something stops me.

"I mean it, though. It depends on what you've heard. I'm doing the only thing I can think to do to keep us safe."

"You call absconding to who knows where keeping us safe? Or is there someone outside the family you're trying to keep safe? Luca," he adds with a soft chuckle completely devoid of warmth that would put any soldier on high alert. "Come on now. You know me better than that. I know where you've been, hanging out in Brooklyn until all hours. I know who lives in Brooklyn. I know who Vitali is trying to get his hands on. And I'm telling you, you need to step out of the way and let it happen. Whoever she is, she's no good for us."

I don't know what's worse—absorbing his disappointment or grappling with the fact that he's been onto me for days. "This is my situation to settle," I defend, standing by my actions.

"Do you realize keeping this girl from him and from your brother, who would also like to speak with her, is the same as pouring gasoline on a fire? It's a fire that's already raging," he reminds me, his voice clipped. "I would hope my son would help us rather than make things worse. No, I don't know who that girl is. I don't know who she is to you. But I know we can't afford her. So, if you thought you would play the hero today and rescue her, I'm sorry to say you wasted your time."

And that's when it hits me. Why did it take so long? "That wasn't one of Vitali's men who went to take care of her today, was it?" I whisper, gripping the phone tighter while she continues splashing in the tub.

He releases a weary sigh. "Son. It's for the best. You'll see that. You know it's not personal, but I have a family to protect, and this is how it needs to be done. I hired a freelancer to follow you to her apartment yesterday, and he returned today but never reported back. What are you doing, sneaking around?"

"What do you know about her?" I ask, needing to understand what the fuck he's getting at.

There he was, pretending to be clueless. I used to respect my father's ability to lie as smoothly as a hot knife cuts through butter.

"Only that she is a liability you've managed to tangle yourself with for too long."

Does he know she's a detective?

Fuck me, I have no idea.

I never imagined his skill at lying would bite me in the ass this way. I must be delusional. "I'm taking care of things. Let me do what I feel is right. The family is in no danger," I reassure him.

"When did you get the idea that it's up to you to decide whether our family is safe?" he asks. "That's up to me to decide, and you could not have picked a worse time to lose focus."

"I haven't."

"If you know what's good for you, you will return immediately. We will have this out, you and I."

"And the girl?" I ask.

His heavy sigh is enough of an answer before he says a word. "Why do you ask questions you already know the answer to, son? Don't let me down."

With that, he ends the call, and it takes everything in me not to throw my cell into the fire. *Motherfucker.* Is he right? Have I completely lost sight of what matters?

There's a louder question in my head, drowning out the others. How do I keep Emilia alive while wrestling with the question of why it's so damn important that I do so? She's been more trouble than she's worth from the beginning. Killing her would solve many problems.

I should do it.

Now.

Tonight.

Yet something deep inside won't allow it. I don't know why. It means going against my father, *my family.* All for the sake of a woman who is terrified of me and would happily take down my entire world.

11

EMILIA

At first, when I heard him talking while I was in the shower, I thought maybe he was talking to himself. He's clearly insane, and I wouldn't put anything past him. For all I know, this isn't a safe house at all. It could be the place where he takes his victims—the ones he wants to get to know a little better before killing them rather than getting it over with quickly.

Now, having gotten out of the tub in more pain than I felt when I first got in, I sense it was a real conversation on the phone, and one he is not happy about the outcome.

I was already shivering on exiting the steamy shower, but the temperature throughout the cabin seems to have dropped by the time I step into the living room dressed in nothing but the towel wrapped around me. Luca hardly glances my way. A definite change from the erection he was sporting before I retreated to the bathroom.

The sight should've scared me, but all it did was turn my insides to lava, especially considering the way his eyes crawled over my body. The magma has cooled thanks to the icy glance he shoots my way once he notices me. "You need to go to bed," he announces, cold and dismissive.

Why is my immediate reaction one of excitement? The briefest sizzle of heat ripples over my bare skin, and I hate myself for it. *This is the man who kidnapped me. Not the man I should want, ever.* "Excuse me?" I whisper.

"What part of that was so difficult to understand?" All of the desire that was practically pulsing in the air earlier is gone. I may as well have imagined it. Now, there's nothing but seething hatred. "Bed. I have a lot on my mind, and you shouldn't push me right now."

It's not so much his warning that tightens my chest until it's difficult to breathe. It's the sight of his fists loosening and tightening rhythmically at his sides. He's losing it, and I can't stop it from happening.

He must be in trouble for bringing me here. He mentioned something about his brother wanting to talk to me, didn't he? *Dante.* He'll be pissed. Is that who was on the phone?

I fold my arms over my chest, and my teeth chatter when a rush of air passes over me. That's not for show, either. The cabin is cold and drafty, even with a fire burning, but my fear is what's chilled me. "Are you coming with me? Is that what this is about?"

"Stop talking." He wraps a hand around my elbow and drags me to the bedroom, ignoring my pained cry as my leg protests. "I brought your bag in. Put some clothes on and be grateful. That's what I'm ordering you to do, *Detective.*"

I feel control slipping through my fingers. It was an illusion, really. The idea of having power. "You're scaring me." Because why not? I need to reach the part of him that likes hearing that. *Besides, it's true.*

He is unmoved. If anything, his scowl turns into a

snarl. "Stop telling me things I already know, Detective. Now move your pretty ass, put on some clothes, and get into bed. Don't make me tie you down," he threatens, and I know it isn't empty. I have no doubt he would follow through just to watch me squirm.

As promised, my bag sits at the foot of a queen-size bed with a metal frame and what looks to be cheap, thin pillows stacked at the head. "I guess I shouldn't bother asking how you knew where to find a bag to pack me up," I murmur, recalling how familiar he was with my apartment.

He doesn't say anything, too busy filling the room with his resentment.

"You could have killed me whenever you wanted to," I remind him in a soft voice. I wish I could say the little tremble in my voice is faked, something to boost his ego and get him excited, but that would be a lie. I'm only human, and this man has clearly stalked me for days. I was at his mercy and didn't know it.

When I finish locating pajamas and underwear, I look up from the small pile of clothes and straight into his cold, hard eyes. He's got that disconnected look, the same one he wore back at the apartment moments after he took that man's life.

The hair rises on the back of my neck, and goose bumps pebble my arms and legs. At least I can use that to my advantage, shivering a little, rubbing my arms, and doing everything I can to appear vulnerable. My leg is screaming from hip to knee, and I can barely stand to look at it when I purposely drop my towel. I hate to do this, but it's the only way to get him to come back around. I pretend to examine the ugly purple skin while Luca stares at me. *Please, come back around.*

Without even looking at him, the heat from his gaze sears my skin. He can't come up with ways to hurt me when he's busy planning to fuck me. I can handle him better that way.

As it stands now? This is Luca Santoro at his most unpredictable.

And deadly.

"It could've been worse," he remarks with a grunt that sounds close to an accusation as he watches me gently touch the edges of the bruise. "And you still haven't thanked me."

The reminder only confuses me. "I still don't understand why," I counter. "Why did you stop me? We wouldn't be going through any of this if you hadn't."

I look up to find his eyes glued to my breasts, and I wish I could say the desire burning in his dark eyes didn't turn me on a little. When he catches me watching him, his gaze hardens along with the rest of his face. He's fighting what he wants most, and it's pissing him off. "I'm not in the business of explaining myself to anybody, including you, Detective," he growls out. "Now, put some fucking clothes on before I make you wish you had."

Rather than continue to bang my head against the wall, I dress as quickly as possible, considering I'm basically balanced on one leg most of the time. He doesn't offer to help. In fact, he releases a derisive snort when I suck in a pained breath and stumble a little. "Remember..." he taunts, "... none of this would be happening if you hadn't—"

"Tried to do my job?" Dammit, I need to be better at controlling myself, but there are limits to anybody's endurance. The fact that he has the nerve to lecture me makes me want to scream as it is.

"Is that what you call it?"

"What else would I call it?" I ask in a much more

straightforward, less accusatory way. I widen my eyes, innocent and confused. "I was doing my job."

"The way I was doing mine," he insists with a growl that turns my blood cold.

We have very different ideas about that, but I'm not about to start an argument. "You think it's easy for me?" I ask, sitting on the bed, letting my hair hang in front of my face while I stare down at my clasped hands. Is he going to buy this? Do I have a choice but to try?

His derisive snort doesn't inspire confidence. "My sympathies don't lie with you, Detective."

"Right," I whisper, nodding. "You kept me alive for this. So you could make me regret trying to infiltrate your club."

"See? You do get the idea eventually. I thought you never would."

"But you don't get it."

"And I don't care, either," he snaps.

I flinch but continue anyway, "You don't know what it's like, always having to prove myself and being the one who is ignored. Or worse, the person whose ideas are ignored until they come out of somebody else's mouth, somebody who is taller and louder and a man."

He yawns loudly. "Is there a point to this? Are you unburdening yourself? Clearing your conscience before I kill you?"

"I was only trying to prove myself." This train of thought started as a means of gaining sympathy and maybe a little trust, yet now I'm really tearing up. The frustration I've fought against since the day I started at the academy wells up in my chest, tightening it, filling me with despair I usually keep in check. It's unusual to allow myself to give in to it, but I don't have a choice now that I've started. I can't hold it back.

"If you think this is going to change my mind, you're wasting your breath." He steps up to the foot of the bed, only inches from where I shiver in this dark, cold room. "I've heard much more heartrending confessions from people I cared a hell of a lot more about than I do you. And they never help. So don't bother with the sob story."

"You should've let me step in front of the car." I run a hand under my nose, pissed at myself for crying and hating him even more for being the reason why. "It would've been merciful."

"I don't do mercy." I believe him, and the sick certainty makes me want to curl up and die. Either he's going to use me as a fuck toy before discarding me, or he's going to murder me straight out. What have I got to live for?

Yourself. The voice is small and weak but clear, nonetheless. I have to win. There has to be a way. I can't swallow the idea that he'd go to all this trouble to keep me alive, only to turn around and kill me. That must be what he's telling himself to justify going against the family.

I need to cling to that hope and never let go. Otherwise, I don't know what will crush me first—the despair or disappointment in myself every time my body betrays me by reacting to his nearness.

He waits until the sniffling has stopped before speaking. "Lie down." He's softer now. Not gentle, but no longer murderous, either. New hope flickers to life in my chest and loosens some of the tightness. I might have gotten through to him, at least for now.

I peer up at him through my wet, snarled hair. He's breathing harder, his lips parted, his nostrils flared. This sick fuck. Turned on by my misery.

But he's not the only one with a problem once our eyes meet, and a blistering heat erupts in my core. *What does that say about me?*

"Is there a problem here?" He makes me flinch when he steps closer, then pulls back the blankets before grasping my shoulders. "When I tell you to do something, you do it. Understood?"

"Y-yes?" I choke out now that my throat has closed to the size of a pinhole.

"Is that a question, or are you agreeing?" I groan when the pressure from his hands turns painful. "Determined to push me, aren't you?"

"No." I doubt he hears me, not that I'm telling the truth. I *was* pushing him, seeing how far I could go. And now I know.

I regret it as his fingers bite into my shoulders. He shoves me back until I'm flat, struggling with the adrenaline pumping through my system and trying to regain my balance. He knocks the breath from my lungs when he lands on top of me. He's breathing hard, glaring at me, his teeth bared in a snarl. I twist and turn, trying to fight him off of me, but that only makes him press his weight into me further.

"Don't." He sneers, grabbing both my wrists and pinning them with concrete force above my head. I wince at the force.

He looks me over as if he's sizing me up, and the disdain he wears tells me he's unimpressed. "I should have let that car flatten you. You fucked up everything for me. Why did you have to do that?"

I can hardly pull air into my lungs, with his weight nearly crushing me. "I wasn't—"

"Like hell you weren't!" Spit flies from his mouth and hits my cheeks. I turn my face, whimpering, wildly afraid that this is my last night on Earth. This is where I die, and no one will ever know what happened to me. I should have fought harder. I shouldn't have made it so easy for him.

"Let's get one thing straight." His hand snaps to my jaw, turning my head so we're eye to eye. He leans in close enough that our noses touch, and there's not so much as a hint of heat or desire now. The only thing my body knows is fear. "Stop lying to me. You entered my life so you could destroy it. Enough of this '*I was just doing my job*' bullshit. Understood? Say it. Tell me you understand," he demands, his breaths coming heavier.

"I understand." I can't fight him when he has me pinned like this or talk my way out of it when I can hardly suck in enough air to remain conscious. All I can do is look him in the eye. He has stripped away my sense of security, my sense of who I am, and what I'm capable of. But he will not strip away my dignity.

No matter how he tries.

"I ought to fuck you to death," he whispers. "Split you in half. At least I would get something out of this bullshit." A slow, knowing smile stirs his finely crafted lips. "And don't pretend the idea doesn't do something for you, Detective." He rolls his hips, forcing his covered erection against my mound, and I hate him for it because, *oh, God*, it feels good.

Like something I want.

No, need.

Nothing he's said or done has lessened my insatiable craving for him. If anything, I want him more. Rather, my body does, heating, moistening, and melting against his firm, unforgiving muscles. My back arches before I know what I'm doing, and I shudder when my tight nipples brush his chest through our clothes. The impulse to spread my legs and welcome him is intense enough to make disbelieving tears well in my eyes.

I shouldn't want this. I should scream, kick, claw, and spit on this monster. This killer. My flailing sense of self-worth pulls up the memory of him in his office, holding a hammer coated in blood. I cannot forget what he's capable of.

Though the memory is foggy and faint enough that I can almost pretend I imagined it. That's the hold Luca has on me. It's what's going to get me killed if I'm not careful —letting down my guard, letting go of everything I am in hopes that he'll touch me.

And he knows it.

His smile widens as a wicked gleam sparkles in his eyes. "I thought so," he murmurs, then raises himself away from me, off the bed, leaving me shaking, wanting, and hating us both. "Now go to sleep. I have shit to take care of."

He leaves the door open, and I hear his feet hitting the floor for what seems like hours, pacing like a caged animal.

How much longer before the animal attacks?

12

LUCA

I should kill her.

She doesn't mean shit. *Right?* She's already gotten in my way. I've neglected the club and my responsibilities to the family.

All for her.

I know that will be the first question out of everyone's mouths when we reconnect once this is over.

How will it all end?

I don't know. I only know that it must, at some point, be the way everything ends. I can't live the rest of my days in limbo.

So why can't I get it over with? It would be so easy. A bullet to her pretty head, maybe somewhere out in the woods where the animals will take care of what's left. Nobody comes out here. If she ever was, it would be ages before humans found her.

There would be no problems with the police. I am always careful never to leave fingerprints, and the freelancer my father sent to the apartment wore gloves as well. A piece of shit building like that sure as hell didn't have security cameras mounted anywhere. There's no proof of us having anything to do with her.

We are safe.

So why does the thought of leaving her body here to rot fill me with so much dread? Hell, I didn't feel this way when I found out about Frankie. There was that moment of shock when grief washed over me, and I saw everything laid bare. All the times I made excuses for him, covered up for his lack of discipline, poor habits, and poorer judgment, part of me knew it might end that way. Deep down, I knew Papa was right. He was always going to be a liability.

You'd think I would know better by now than to let a liability drag me down. I rid myself of one that night, only for another to immediately take its place.

It's enough to make me laugh in disbelief, shaking my head as I pound my fist into my open palm and turn on my heel, prepared to walk the length of the living room again. There isn't much space to cover, meaning I've paced in tight ovals long enough for the fire to die down until it's barely more than a few weak flames licking at what's left of the wood.

I take a few logs from the wood pile beside the fireplace and toss them inside, willing the fire to catch and grow. Gripping the mantle, my mind refuses to settle. There shouldn't be a choice here, yet I can't seem to commit.

What is it about her? She's nothing, she's no one, and unless I'm careful, she'll get me killed. I know better than this.

I know what I need to do.

She is in bed right now.

Why don't you go and do it?

My fists clench, and I grind my teeth, looking from the fireplace to the open bedroom door. Is she asleep? I wouldn't be surprised if she were lying there, cursing herself the way I plague myself.

The way she reacted to me left me disappointed. I could practically smell her arousal. She wanted to give herself to me, wanted it with everything in her. I held back thanks to what was left of my good sense stopping me. I know with what's left of my soul that fucking her would only take a shit situation and make it worse. It's bad enough, the way I've wanted to claim her all this time. Once I do, there won't be any hope of getting out of this unscathed.

Kill her. Claim her. Abandon her. Fuck her. On and on it goes, my head spinning as the conflict rages. I grip the mantle tighter as if my grasp on it will help firm the hold I have over myself, as if that will help somehow.

"I need to use the bathroom."

My head snaps up at the sound of her voice, and something in me rejoices at how she falls back a step when she sees what I can only imagine is rage embedded across my features—anger at her, at myself. I could snap her neck easily, quickly. She wouldn't suffer.

My blood simmers at the sight of the fear in her eyes. She's right to be afraid. It might be the smartest, most authentic impulse she's had so far. She should be frightened of me.

She takes a tentative step beyond the bedroom, chewing her lip. All I do is watch in silence, tracing the curves of her body with my hungry gaze, noting the way she limps. She'll be feeling that now, lying still for so long.

Good.

Let her suffer a little, the way she's made me suffer

The way I have let myself suffer over her.

"Leave the door open," I growl out before she can close it. She hesitates, staring at the floor, but she's smart enough to release the doorknob and turn away, limping to the toilet. I have no desire to watch her. That's never been my thing, but I loom in the doorway just the same and smile when her face goes beet red.

"You're going to watch me?" she questions quietly, staring at the floor.

"What a smart little detective you are."

"Is this what gets you off?" There's a tremor in her voice, but her gaze is unflinching when she lifts her eyes to meet mine.

"What gets me off is my business. Now do what you need and be grateful you've got more than a bucket to piss in." Her chin quivers, but she offers no reply, quickly dropping her yoga pants to her knees, along with the tiny thong she wears underneath. She stares at the wall opposite the toilet, shaking with what I imagine is either rage or shame. Maybe both.

Watching her shouldn't stir such deep satisfaction in my soul, but I find myself lighting up, craving more. "Look at the brave little detective now," I muse, folding my arms and leaning against the door. The way she flinches makes me laugh. "Have you learned your lesson yet?"

"What's the lesson?" She wipes quickly but tries to stand faster than her body is capable of balancing her. She stumbles, barely managing to grab the tub's edge to catch herself.

"You aren't invincible. You aren't all that strong. You thought you were. You thought you could do what people have tried for generations to accomplish, and you were going to do it all on your own."

"You hate me for that, don't you?"

I hate her for so many things, I wouldn't know where to begin listing them all. "For starters," I mutter, watching as she washes her hands. She meets the gaze reflected at her in the mirror and runs her wet fingers through her tangled hair. Then she splashes her face before staring at herself again.

"What are you thinking?" I taunt, enjoying the way she tenses at my question. "Are you wondering how long it would take to find shelter when you don't have the first idea of our location? Maybe you're asking yourself how to get hold of my car keys. Or maybe, *just maybe,* you're wondering if I'll stop myself the next time I have you pinned to a bed."

"Stop," she growls out, almost baring her teeth at her own reflection.

"Who are you talking to? Me, or yourself? Because some things can't be excused away so easily. Such as how desperate you are for me."

"Stop saying that," she whispers, her usual bite absent.

Unlikely. This is what gets through to Emilia—more than pain and the threat of dying. *That* she can handle. Being accused of wanting my cock, on the other hand? She wants to spit nails, and I might be insulted if I didn't know she was lying to herself. "Do you mean to tell me you would fight me off if I bent you over that sink right now?"

"You won't."

"And you know this how?"

"Because you would've done it by now if that was what you planned to do." She stands up straight, tucking her hair behind both ears before lifting her chin.

Dear God, why does that slight gesture stiffen my dick the way it does? The last thing I want from her is some misguided, childish sense of strength to rear its head. Like I don't have enough complications to deal with already.

All it takes is a glimpse of the fire in her blue eyes to awaken every predatory instinct I've spent my life trying to manage. Now I'm a cat toying with a mouse it has cornered, and my pulse picks up speed in anticipation of what could be fun. There is so much I need to consider, so much I should be planning. But this is a diversion, and one I desperately need.

I lunge toward her, pressing the small of her back against the sink. She leans away until the back of her head touches the mirror, breathing fast, her body stiff. I know from experience it won't be that way for long, and she confirms this by trembling when I run my hand down her side.

"What about now?" I whisper, leaning in close, inhaling the sweetness of her hair and skin and tuning in to her rapid, shallow breaths. "Here we are. Me against you, you against the sink. What are you going to do about it? Because from where I'm standing…"

She grinds her teeth together when I cup her tit, molding it against my palm, closing my eyes to absorb the feel of it—the firmness, the weight, and that tight nipple brushing against my palm. "From where I'm standing, you are a heartbeat away from begging for me."

"Keep telling yourself that," she grunts out.

"I have to give it to you. You're damn determined to keep up the act."

"You haven't figured out yet that it's not an act?"

"Isn't it?" I ask with a humorless laugh before upping the ante.

Her gasp rings out sharp and loud when I thrust a hand between her thighs to cup her sex. Her mouth falls open, and her features soften. Yes, this is what she wants, what we both want, what we've always wanted since the club. If things had gone differently that night, I would've fucked her until she swore she was hit by a hurricane. I might never have let her out of my bed.

"Say it again," I croon close to her ear, grinning at the

way she shivers when my breath hits her skin. "Tell me this isn't what you want. Come on, Detective. Lie to me. I dare you."

"It's not a lie." Her blue eyes hold mine in her delivery. There is a heat behind them, heat that does something to me.

"Isn't it?" I press my fingers against her warm flesh, massaging her clit through her clothes, laughing when she slaps weekly at my shoulders.

Like that would stop me.

"Drop the act," I whisper against her ear before running my tongue along the seashell curve of her lobe. She gasps, then does exactly what I knew she would do. She parts her legs and bears down on my hand.

And she begins to grind.

Now I wonder if I've made a mistake because if I get much harder, I'll break the zipper on my pants. Her breath is warm against my neck, hot and frantic. Every grind of her hips marks a bit more of herself she's willing to give to me, one step further away from whoever she thinks she is. And this is why I can't bring myself to end her life. The thrill of satisfaction, knowing I was right, that she sees me clearly but still can't deny what her body needs. I could become addicted to it.

I might already have.

"Are you going to come for me?" I growl as I press harder, rubbing her clit while she whimpers and moans.

"No... no!" Her weak protests fall on deaf ears.

"Tell me to stop," I whisper before nipping her earlobe and savoring her helpless cries. She's soaked through her thong and pants, and the fabric molds itself to her lips. "Just tell me to stop, Emilia. Tell me to stop before I make you come."

"You... you have to..." It's a plea, a sob, but it still isn't enough to make her quit the slow, rhythmic grinding against the heel of my hand.

"That's not quite good enough. Make me stop. Do it if that's what you really want."

"I… I…" Then she gasps, and one of her hands finds the back of my head before her fingers thread through my hair and tug hard while her body shudders in release.

She never stood a chance.

I have to force myself to step back when every part of me demands I keep going. I don't want to stop at a single orgasm. It's not enough to smell her arousal on my hand. I need to taste, to drive my tongue between those plump lips and lap up every drop of her.

When her eyes open to meet mine, there's a simple truth behind them. She wants the same thing. My cock is hard enough it's painful, and she is so tempting, willing even, but I won't. Because once I do, it will be that much more impossible for this to end.

And it has to end.

"Clean up that wet pussy," I mutter as I back away, noting how she trembles under the weight of my stare.

Her body sags a little against the sink as she lowers her head. "You're a bastard," she whispers.

I've been called much worse, but hearing it from her makes me tick. "The bastard who just made you come… and you're welcome for that," I add, snickering when she flinches in shame. "Go back to bed once you're clean. Don't make me tell you again."

I could join her. I should lie beside her to make sure she doesn't move or sneak out of the room and do anything stupid. The thing is, I can't trust myself, knowing the temptation would be too much to ignore if we were that close. It's safer to stretch out on the sofa, fully dressed.

I don't bother to take off my shoes. At a time like this,

it's always best to be prepared to move. Considering I am no closer to deciding my next steps, there's always the chance we'll have to make a run for it.

And the fact that I think of it as *we* rather than *I* doesn't give me much comfort.

13

EMILIA

I'm going to die.

I can't reach my gun, and I'm going to die.

The floor is so slippery, and I can't get up. I can't stop what's about to happen. No matter how I stretch and strain to reach the gun, it keeps sliding farther away. There's nowhere to hide from the giant in the doorway, so tall, broad, and looming over me.

His thin lips stretch in a sick smile.

And he pulls the trigger.

"No! Stop!"

My eyes snap open in a strange room where I'm wrapped in inky darkness. My muscles are frozen. I can't move. I can hardly breathe. There isn't a sound except for the fading echo of the scream that woke me—*my scream*—and the heavy pounding of my heart.

"Emilia?" Luca runs into the room, breathless, before almost draping himself over me. It all comes rushing back in a sickening wave. I'm in the cabin. I was only dreaming about the events of this afternoon going much differently than they did.

He reaches over and turns on a small lamp to cast a

warm glow over the room. Being able to see goes a long way toward breaking me out of the paralysis that gripped me after I woke up. Now that I can see his face, the concern etched across his features is evident when he leans over me again. "You screamed," he whispers, his dark eyes wide and searching.

"I was having a nightmare." Now, I feel the wetness on my cheeks and the pillow. I was crying. Luca Santoro has discovered me crying in bed like a baby. My humiliation knows no bounds. I run a hand over my cheeks, resenting the tears that make me look weak.

I can't afford that.

I can't look at him.

The thought of looking at my reflection the next time I go to the bathroom is something I can barely stomach. How can I look myself in the eyes after what I allowed to happen hours ago? I let him humiliate me. Hell, I practically begged him to do it and gave him the keys to my body. He knows how much I want him. There's no use pretending otherwise now. I have completely lost what little leverage I had. I'm weak, he knows it, and I don't have the first clue what happens next.

My only hope—small, like a tiny flame in the darkness —lies in whatever he feels for me. He talks like he wants to hurt me, but he hasn't yet. Not really. Aside from a little rough groping, he's left me unharmed. Physically, anyway. Emotionally? That's another story for when I have the time to get into it.

I'm so weary. My limbs feel heavy when I shift my weight on the mattress. The only sleep I managed to get came in short, light bursts, and the few dreams I managed were gory, bloody, a little too close to reality, like my most recent nightmare.

He sits back, giving me space but stopping short of

leaving me alone. "You scared the shit out of me." He releases a dry, shaky laugh. "Fuck. The last thing you want to hear when you're in the middle of nowhere in the middle of the night is a scream like that."

It must be the fact that he's looking a little disheveled and vulnerable that gives me the balls to say it. "Like that's the first scream you've ever heard."

At first, his brows draw together in a stern expression. It soon fades before a faint smile passes over his lips. "I make women scream, but not that way," he assures me in a voice dripping with innuendo.

He would turn it into something sexual, wouldn't he? "That's not what I meant," I mutter, rolling my eyes.

"No shit," he deadpans. "You think I'm the guy who got off on torturing bugs and small animals when I was a kid? I'll have you know I didn't torture my first animal until I was sixteen."

"What?" I whisper, horror-struck.

"Jesus, you're gullible." He laughs, and it's a nice sound. It reminds me of the man I met at the club that first night—charming and warm enough to make me laugh softly along with him. Once he's gone quiet, he pins me in place with a penetrative stare. "What were you dreaming about?"

I roll onto my back and blow out a sigh. Luca might not be into torturing animals, but he's not above torturing me with questions I'd rather not answer. It'll only get worse if I shut down. "Today. Or yesterday, I guess. In my bathroom."

"You're a big, bad detective, right?" he asks with a snort. "You shouldn't get so shaken up by something like that."

All his smartass comment earns him is a withering look from me. "There's a difference between being on the job and falling out of the tub, completely naked and unarmed and already wounded," I snap.

"Watch it." Darkness creeps back into his voice, and it brings ice along with it. "I'm sitting here, trying to take your mind off your nightmare, and you get a shitty attitude with me?"

With my kidnapper.

My kidnapper, who saved my life.

I'll never unravel this entire fucked-up situation, not if I had a hundred years to try. "It's been a difficult twenty-four hours." Including the fact that he basically assaulted me in the bathroom earlier, no matter how much I liked it.

"For both of us," he reminds me before standing, and I wish my heart wouldn't sink like it does. I shouldn't want him to stay with me.

I can't trust him not to use my body for his amusement the way he did earlier.

I can't trust myself not to want him to, either.

My skin crawls and erupts in goose bumps all at the same time when I remember coming for him.

Rather than leave me alone, though, he rounds the bed and sits on the other side. "What are you doing?" I whisper, almost breathless with confusion, once he stretches out beside me.

"Relax," he mutters, punching the pillows before resting his head on them. "That sofa is about as comfortable as sleeping on a bare floor, and I'd rather you not wake me from the little sleep I manage to get by screaming like a banshee."

"I could still scream," I warn him, freezing up again. To think, I was comforted by his presence until now. "I'll scream the walls down."

"Go ahead." He folds his hands on top of his flat stomach, ankles crossed. He's still wearing his shoes. When he catches me looking, he mutters, "In case we need to move fast. It's not a good idea to be completely vulnerable."

"You think we'd have to move fast?" I ask, forgetting my apprehension in the face of something more important. This man is dangerous, but there are others far more deadly. Like the one I met earlier today who would have murdered me if Luca hadn't shown up.

"There's never any way of knowing." He yawns loudly, then sighs. "I'm beat. Turn out the light."

Red flags are everywhere. "Can we leave it on?" I ask, still frozen in place. Having him this close is doing terrible things to my mind and body, which are currently at war over how to feel about this turn of events. My chest is tight enough that I have to fight for every breath, yet my nipples are hard as bullets at the memory of how easy it was for him to make me shatter around him earlier.

I wanted him.

I wanted more.

I still do, and I hate myself for it. I hate him even more, even if he did seem genuinely worried when he first came in.

"Don't be a child," he murmurs as his eyes slide shut. "Turn it off. There's nothing I could do to you with it off that I couldn't do while it's on."

There's a lovely thought that will surely help me get back to sleep.

When I hesitate, he groans and rolls onto his side, facing me. "I'm here with you," he reminds me in a quiet, weary voice. "Nobody will hurt you. And if it seems like you're having a bad dream, I'll wake you up. No need for the nightlight."

My pride rears up at the word he chose. "A nightlight? Fuck off," I grumble before reaching across the nightstand to turn off the lamp. At least he tries to hide his snide laughter, but he's not trying hard.

"You're a little too easy to predict, *Detective*," he taunts as usual, the word drops from his lips like a curse.

"Don't break your arm patting yourself on the back," I retort, and he only snickers in the darkness. Is this happening? Am I bickering with my kidnapper? A vicious murderer, cruel and violent and cold.

Yet he came running when he heard me scream.

I shouldn't waste time trying to understand him, but I can't help wanting to. Maybe I need to. It's my only means of maintaining an illusion of control over my situation. If I know my captor, I can predict what he'll do. I might be able to get through to the sliver of humanity he still possesses and save my life.

"Go to sleep," he murmurs in a softer voice than before. "You'll be fine now. You aren't alone."

I'm sure he thinks he's comforting me, and this brief flash of decency and kindness will erase the harm he's done. How much he's hurt me.

You wouldn't be going through this if it wasn't for the chance you took at the club. Right. Like that reminder makes me feel any better.

With the lights off, it means he can't see the tears that roll down both sides of my face at his rather weak attempt to comfort me. He thinks I'm not alone?

I've never felt more alone in my life.

14

LUCA

I t's been three days alone with her.

Three days of trying to ignore phone calls from Papa and Dante.

"It'll be easier to play poker when we have a deck with all fifty-two cards," I point out with a sigh as I study the hand Emilia has presented, then compare it with my pitiful pair of threes.

She snorts, rolling her eyes. "You could just admit I'm a better player. I still managed a straight without all the cards being available."

"Brag all you want." I leave the table, almost glad for an excuse to go after she's kicked my ass all morning. "I'll grab a fresh deck when I'm out, and then we'll see who's bragging."

"Ooh, see if there are any paperbacks at the store," she asks tentatively when I shoot her a glare. "I've already been through most of what you found tucked around the cabin." Her gaze falls on the small stack of books sitting on the coffee table. I've also been through most of them if only to distract myself from the increasingly fraught situation I've placed myself in.

"I'll keep an eye out," I grunt out as I put on my coat, and her smile leaves me, determined to stop at a bookstore if I have to. So long as she keeps smiling, and the warmth in my chest reminds me why I still haven't taken her back to Long Island as the family thinks I should.

It's bizarre but no less true. I'm a different man when I leave the cabin to head out for supplies than when we first arrived.

I have to shake my head and laugh at the corny direction my thoughts have taken as I pull away from the cabin on a bitterly cold afternoon. She's watching from the window, and part of me wants to slam on the brakes and stay here rather than risk leaving her alone, knowing she could easily run away.

Not so easily. I have to remind myself of that, and it's the only thing that keeps me moving. After she was struck by that car, it's still painful for her to get around. How do I know? Aside from the way she winces and gasps, especially after she's been sitting or lying down for a while, she lets me help her. That's how I know she's suffering. Rather than shove me away or pretend she's stronger than she is, she allows me to walk her around the cabin while she leans against me. It must grate on her ass to admit she's anything less than strong and fully capable.

Mobility issues, combined with the fact that she has no idea where we are, would make it highly improbable for an intelligent person like her to make a stupid choice like running away. If she's going to survive, she needs me. She needs to stay where she is.

What a shame the risk of taking her with me far outweighs the risk of leaving her here.

Dressed in the clothes I found in the dresser and closet,

I blend in easily once I reach the shopping district roughly equidistant from the cabin and the ski resorts further up the mountain. We believe in preparing for all possibilities, including a long stay, which has come in handy.

I can't afford to take long on my errands and risk exposure. With that in mind, I keep a sharp eye out as I roll through the parking lot in front of a grocery store. There are a few plates from New York and several from New Jersey. I don't recognize any of them. My father must have guys out looking for me by now, but there's nothing around to set off my instincts.

Twenty minutes later, I leave the store with a bag of groceries in each arm, careful to go about my business without attracting attention but always watching in case there's already someone around here looking for me. By the time I'm on the road again, my pulse has picked up speed, and I find myself making a conscious effort to stay close to the speed limit. That's all I need, getting pulled over at a time like this.

It isn't so much that I'm in a hurry to make sure Emilia doesn't try to run. It's more that I can't wait to get back to her. That's why I'm in a hurry. She's what I crave. The forty minutes we've been apart have been too long already. This is what she's done to me and who she's turned me into. Or maybe I'm who I've turned myself into since I was already addicted to her well before I killed for her.

By the time I turn off the main road and onto the narrow, half-hidden lane leading to the cabin, my heart's ready to burst out of my chest. According to her, the one thing she craves more than anything right now is spaghetti, garlic bread, and ice cream, all three of which are waiting for her in the back seat. She'll smile and be happy, all because of me.

I can't wait.

As usual, I park behind the cabin, then carry the bags around the cabin and through the front door. "They had chocolate peanut butter and cookie dough," I call out as I step inside and kick the door closed behind me, then cross the room to leave the bags on the kitchen table. "I wasn't sure which you'd like better, so I got both."

That's how long it takes me to realize I'm alone in the cabin. The bathroom door is open, and the room is empty. Same with the bedroom.

Motherfucker. Incredible how little it takes for my buoyant mood to crash.

"Emilia?" I dart to the front door, fling it open, stepping onto the small porch with my head on a swivel. Did somebody come for her while I was gone? It was always a possibility, yet there was no sign of a struggle in the cabin. She would have fought like hell—unless she was wounded, but then blood would be left behind.

She's gone. She left on her own.

A sick feeling slams into me in time with the spike of adrenaline that floods my system. I want to run, hunt, catch, and drag her back. But I can't go off half-cocked. I know that much, even as my head spins and betrayal soaks into my marrow. For three days, she's pretended to soften up toward me. We've spent time reading books left around the cabin, playing cards, and watching television. We've developed a sort of wary camaraderie, all for her to stab me in the fucking back like the traitor she's always been. How could I let myself forget?

I rush back into the cabin, the groceries forgotten in favor of opening the bottom drawer beneath the sink to reveal a safe where I've stored the weapons to keep them away from her. The Glock is waiting for me, and I withdraw it, tucking it into my waistband and growling as I imagine using it on her the way I should've done in the first place.

I stand and turn, prepared to hunt to my dying breath if that's what it takes. Emilia couldn't have gotten far, but with no idea which direction she was headed, it could have taken a while. She'll be lucky if she freezes to death out there. It would be a more merciful death than the one I have in mind.

She lied to me and pretended we were in this together, sleeping side by side, all for her to run. Being with me is apparently worse than freezing to death with the smell of approaching snow in the air.

The front door sits open, and I head that way, teeth gritted, my head pounding with every step I take. Suddenly, she appears like magic, slowly and awkwardly climbing the steps up to the porch with a bundle of sticks and twigs in her arms. When she sees me, she drops them at my feet with a weary groan. "You're finally back. You have no idea what I went through to gather this."

The fog of rage that's wrapped itself around my skull won't allow her words to penetrate. "Where the fuck were you?" I bark out, taking her by the arm and hauling her in close.

She gasps, her head snapping back, eyes wide. "What does it look like? You left me here all by myself, and the fire went dead. There was no wood to add to it. I was freezing in there. What was I supposed to do?"

I didn't bring in more wood. I was supposed to take care of her, yet I overlooked that simple chore. Frustration with myself translates to fury at the entire situation before I shake her, snarling. "You were told to stay inside!"

The fear and confusion in her expression harden into something far sharper and fiercer before she bares her teeth in a snarl of her own. "Hello? I had no idea where you were going, no idea how long it would take since I don't have a clue where we are, and I could see my fucking breath in there," she snaps. "Sorry if I thought I might walk around, try to gather what I could. Do you know how painful it was?" As it is, she's standing on one foot, with only the toes of her right foot touching the floorboards. "You left me here to freeze to death for all I know, then you get an attitude with me?"

"Poor you," I growl out before pulling her into the cabin, the wood forgotten in favor of something far more important—making sure I reestablish the rules around here. For both of us. I was too busy floating around like a fucking lovesick idiot to take care of the essentials, and I could have ended up losing her. What if she'd gotten lost? What if she'd been injured again?

I've lost perspective, and it's unforgivable.

"What are you doing?" she demands, limping pitifully across the cabin before I hurl her into the bedroom. She stumbles and falls against the bed with a pained cry, which somehow serves to intensify my rage until I have to clench my teeth against a scream.

Her already wide eyes bulge with fear when I go to the dresser and pull out the belt I left inside when I changed out of the clothes I arrived in. "No. You're out of your fucking mind!" she shouts before stumbling to the door, but I catch her easily, this time throwing her onto the bed. Her scream is soon muffled by the hand I clamp over her mouth once I've pinned her to the mattress with my body.

A fool. That's all I've become. It took three days for me to lose sight of what matters.

Who she is.

Who I am.

I pull my hand back with a hiss when she sinks her teeth into my finger, then grab her jaw and squeeze hard. "You might be right." I growl as she squirms and fights with no hope of escape. "I might be out of my mind, which means you'd better stop fighting unless you want to see what happens when I've been pushed too far." Her ragged breaths and helpless whimpers are almost soothing to my wounded pride. I want more. No, I need more.

My warning doesn't stop her from trying to slap my hands away when I take her wrists and wrap the belt around them. "Stop this!" she begs, but her pleas are weak thanks to my weight, making it hard for her to breathe. "Please, don't do this!"

It's too late for that. I cinch the leather tight enough that it bites into her flesh, then loop the end of the belt around the bed frame above her head and tie it off. No matter how she tugs and struggles, there's no getting free. "Grunt and curse all you want," I taunt before pulling off her sneakers and getting kicked in the leg for my troubles. "You'll pay for that," I tell her, savoring her dismayed groan.

"Why are you doing this?" she demands, but I hear the terror running beneath the façade of strength.

I don't answer, too busy watching her body move beneath her sweater and yoga pants. Yoga pants, which I quickly pull off, followed by her panties. "No. No! No, you fucker!" She kicks and screams, but it's no use. All it gets her is her ankles held tight in my fists and her legs spread open so I can admire her pretty pussy.

This is how it should've been from the start. Instead of going to bed with blue balls every night, I should've been exploring her, living out every dark, needful fantasy born from obsession. I'm in charge here. I call the shots.

She forgot that…

… and so did I.

"I deserve a reward for all the trouble I've gone to for you," I decide, breathless with anticipation while her panicked breaths and furious grunts warm me to my core. "And I've waited too long for it."

"Don't do this, Luca." Tears now roll down her cheeks, soaking into the chestnut hair fanned across the pillow beneath her head. She's completely helpless and at my mercy. And she thinks pleading will get her anywhere?

"Don't do what?" I mock, grinning at her barely stifled sob when I kneel between her legs. "You don't know what I have in mind. Relax. You might enjoy yourself."

Throwing her legs back until they're almost flat against her stomach, I lower my head and breathe deep, inhaling her pussy's musky, addictive aroma. My cock stands at attention, twitching with every ragged breath she takes before I extend my tongue and run it along her seam.

"Oh!" she cries out, and now there's no anger, fear, or rage. It's surprise and pleasure experienced against her will. I do it again, again, lapping at her like a cat laps up cream until the tension holding her body rigid softens and her sweet nectar begins to flow.

Lifting my head, I gaze across the length of her body to find her eyes closed. There are no more tears. There's only the rapid rise and fall of her chest, still encased in too many layers. I release her ankles and chuckle to myself when her legs fall to the sides. She's no longer kicking, so I push up her sweater and bra to reveal her luscious tits. Her pink nipples are rock hard, and a soft brush of my fingertips over the peaks makes her moan and arch her back.

"I think that's enough," I murmur, grinning when her

eyes snap open in surprise. It's so easy to break her down. "You've learned your lesson." Her mouth falls open, eyes darting over my face. "What?" I prompt, still grinning at how obvious she is. "You want me to keep going? Say the word, and I will."

"I…" Her already flushed face goes a deeper red. Caught between what she knows she should say and the truth of what she craves.

"I could always do *this* if you wanted." Without warning, I sink two fingers deep inside her juicy cunt, relishing the wet, sloppy sound it makes. Her eyes close again and her head rolls to the side before a soft sigh tumbles from her parted lips. Fuck, she's tight, gripping my digits. I curl them slightly, massaging her G-spot as I work them in and out, and her hips buck like she's been shocked.

A feral cry tears its way out of her when I withdraw, my fingers coated in her slick juices. "Oh, you wanted me to continue?" I ask through gritted teeth. We're both being tortured here. Every instinct I possess tells me to claim, to devour. It's taking everything I have to hold back.

"Please…" she begs before a broken sob cuts her off.

"Please, what?" I take a few experimental strokes against her clit, laughing softly when she practically shrieks. "Please stop? Please, make me come? You'll have to be more specific, Emilia." There's a wet spot forming beneath her ass by the time I leave her clit alone, making her raise her hips, demanding my touch again.

"I hate you," she whispers even as she fights to find my fingers, to gain the little bit of friction she'll need to achieve release.

"That's not what I want to hear." I lower my head and purse my lips, blowing across the tip of her clit and setting off a guttural moan. To think we've been wasting time playing cards when I could've spent hours doing this. "Tell me what you want. Should I stop? Or should I lick your clit until you coat my chin in your cum?"

"Oh my God!" She's a woman possessed, completely consumed by what I've done to her body. "Yes, yes, please!"

Her reaction leaves me holding onto control for dear life and fighting for every strangled breath. "Please, what?" I demand in a whisper.

"Please, make me come!" She sobs, and I smile in triumph at the sight and sound of her surrender.

Unable to deny her or myself, I quickly do as I threatened, flicking her clit with the tip of my tongue, groaning at the sound of her deafening cries. She plants her feet against the mattress and raises her hips until her pussy grinds against my face in an increasingly frantic rhythm. "Yes, yes!" she gasps out, rubbing her pussy and its juices over my skin, making my aching cock drip. "Yes, Luca, *yes!*"

Her hips jerk upward one last time, and she stiffens before a shriek pierces the air. A flood of fresh juice flows from her all at once, and I catch it on my tongue, greedy for every drop. It belongs to me, after all.

She owes me.

And I'll take what's mine.

By the time I'm finished and she's gone limp, I raise myself and look down at her. Pride floods me when I take in the sight of her splayed-out body and flushed skin. But it's what happens when her eyes flutter open and meet mine that seizes my heart and catches my breath. The naked understanding in them. The intimacy. We've crossed a line together, and I can't fathom going back. There's no imagining a world in which I don't make her do that every day for the rest of my life. There is no living without the taste of her on my tongue.

I intended to teach her a lesson about who is in control around here.

Now, I have to wonder whether she's been in control of me all along.

15

EMILIA

There's only so long I can stay in bed.

But it's safer here, under the blankets, curled up in a ball. He's awake out there. I hear him in the kitchen, opening and closing cabinets. Making breakfast like there's anything normal about the past week we've spent together. He even whistles to himself while he does it.

I wish the sound didn't stir a smile before I realize what I'm doing.

That's the true danger now. Yes, there's always the threat of murder hanging over our heads, though that threat hasn't been voiced in days. It's something I can't afford to forget. More pressing now is the threat of becoming much too close.

The threat of craving him more intensely than ever.

Four days after he tied me up, I could still die from shame at how I begged him. Nothing in the entire world was as important as ending the torment, easing the unbearable tension I was sure would kill me. I should've fought and screamed until I passed out from the effort, especially after he pulled that whole Jekyll and Hyde act on me. He was in a good mood when he left for town, and I was even looking forward to him returning with a few treats after days spent eating canned soup and dry tuna.

His good mood returned that very night, even as I went out of my way to avoid eye contact. I wasn't afraid of him. I was afraid of myself and my weakness for him. I still am. That fear hasn't subsided. No, it's only grown with each passing day. Every time our eyes have met. Every shared meal. The random conversations we've had, though never about his family or mine, but rather ourselves.

He can't remember the last time he's been to the movies but enjoys watching classics in his family's home theater. He broke his arm when he was nine years old after trying and failing to climb the wall bordering his property. While his parents hail from Sicily, he'd rather dig into a Chinese feast than a plate of lasagna.

He's a shrewd card player, a big reader, and he damn near jumped out of his skin when he mistook an old sock on the closet floor for a snake. The memory makes me giggle softly before my throat closes up.

Stop. Don't let yourself do this.

Because there are other factors in play. It isn't all long discussions and reminiscing. I've woken up three times in the middle of the night to hear hushed, tense conversation coming from the living room. Sometimes, I look his way and find him staring at the fire, his brow furrowed, his jaw tight like he's ready to kill somebody. I can't let myself forget who he is and what started this.

Giving in to the despair creeping up in my chest is dangerous, tightening it and causing a stinging sensation to prickle behind my eyes. I've fought so hard to keep from giving into misery, telling myself it's useless and will only make things worse.

Right now, though, alone in bed without Luca's penetrative stare digging into my skull, I can allow myself to feel.

To wish this was over.

To fear it ending.

To know there can't be a scenario in which I make it out alive once his family tracks me down, which they're bound to do.

"Wake up if you haven't already." When his voice rings out, it's surprisingly close to the bedroom door. "I'm making breakfast. It'll be ready in a minute."

For some reason, the pressure of the ticking clock and the reminder of how our time is running out presses down on me, making me question if this is how he does it. Death by poisoning. He can't keep me alive forever, no matter how distressingly friendly things have turned for us.

There are easier ways to get rid of me, I suppose. Quicker too. If only I could get a grasp on why he's going to all the trouble of keeping me alive. It can't be because he wants me. He has his entire family to worry about and the business, all of it. I can't possibly be enough to make him forget what he's been raised to do.

Something that smells like it could be pancakes piques my interest and gets my stomach growling, making the doubt slip away. I'm too hungry to let pride get in the way now. I just wish it didn't feel so much like I was getting ready to go into battle as I sit up and gingerly swing my legs over the edge of the bed, shivering when my bare feet touch the cold floor.

Rather than stay in my pajamas, I change into an oversized sweater and a pair of leggings, trying like hell as I pull them on not to think too much about how easily I spread my legs for him. I'm so ashamed that I could die.

I worked really hard to succeed, never once considering

using my body to get ahead, even when one of my academy instructors called me in late one night, assuring me my fast track to detective should I suck his cock there and then. But now, I did what I swore I'd never do—use my body to get ahead. What's worse is that I didn't push him away, leaving me more confused than ever.

When I finally muster the courage to leave the bedroom, I find him at the stove. He's rolled up the sleeves of his button-down shirt, unbuttoned to reveal a wide expanse of bare chest with the word *Santoro* inked across it. The fresh, clean scent of soap mixes with the pancakes. He must've showered during the short time I was asleep this morning.

It isn't the promise of food that makes my mouth water when he turns my way, holding a plate. It's memories I'm helpless against, and the sight of his chiseled abs isn't helping.

"It's just a boxed mix, eggs, and water, but it's better than nothing." He leaves the plate on the table before turning back to the stove. There's a small bottle of syrup waiting for me along with a fork. No knife, I note. He doesn't trust me enough for that. And I don't blame him.

I can't make this image of a domestic and even slightly cheerful man line up with the monster who ravished me days ago. I'll never forget the look on his face when I found him storming toward me. He was enraged, ready to kill. All because he couldn't find me in the cabin. He thought I ran away as if I would. I'm not suicidal.

Slowly, I lower myself onto one of the hard wooden chairs by the table, wincing at the pain still present in my leg. It's not nearly as sharp anymore, but it's still there, especially first thing in the morning. My hands shake as I cut into the pancakes with the side of my fork before I've even added syrup. They are dry and flavorless, but they're hot and filling. I add syrup and take another huge mouthful, chewing fast before shoveling more in. Nerves have left my appetite spotty at best, but today it's raging.

I'm already halfway through when he sits down across from me with his plate. "I don't do a lot of this," he murmurs, and it's strange. His voice is somehow softer. That edge of resentment is gone, or at least far enough away that it's barely noticeable.

"Kidnapping?" I ask between bites. Maybe I'm more suicidal than I thought since the word came out before I could help it.

He snorts softly. "Something like that." After a mouthful of pancakes, he coughs at their dryness before taking a long drink from a glass of orange juice. "I had to eyeball the measurements," he admits with a wry chuckle.

"This is fine."

"Of course it is. I'm not sure you can taste it. You're eating so fast." Am I imagining the humor in his voice? Is there something funny about this situation? I'm still his captive—pancakes or no pancakes, oral sex or no oral sex.

Yet when he looks up from his plate, our eyes meet, and the corners of his mouth stir like he's trying to suppress a grin. Part of me wants to return it, making me want to scream.

We are not in this together.

We are not partners.

We are not friends.

We are nothing to each other. And there is no reason for me to soften in his presence. An enormous, shattering orgasm isn't going to make me forget who I am or who he is.

"Can I ask you something?" Since he's in a good mood, I may as well see how far I can get. "What's your play here, really?"

"My play?" he asks with a snort. "Where did you pick up your terminology? The police academy?"

"Could you answer my question?" I ask with a weary roll of my eyes.

"It doesn't concern you," he insists.

"You're holding me hostage in a cabin in the middle of the woods. You prevented me from being murdered... twice. I think this concerns me very much."

He lowers his brow. "We'll agree to disagree."

If this blasé attitude is meant to piss me off, he's succeeding. "If you're going to hand me over, why not get it over with? You can't keep me like this forever."

"Be careful." He doesn't miss a beat, cutting another segment of pancake away from the rest, spearing it with his fork, and dragging it through syrup. "I'm not in the mood to fight today, but you could take me there. Understood?"

No. I do not understand because I've never dealt with someone like him before. All I have are questions, fears, none of which are being served by a shitty, if filling, breakfast. He says one thing, then does another. He wants the privilege of ending my life but can't seem to get around to going through with it. Why? If I could only figure that out, I could use it against him. And that's exactly why he won't reveal what's going on in his head. Because once I know, he's toast. And he knows it.

Maybe I can push him hard enough that he'll crack. Do I want to take that chance? Because once he cracks, what happens then? Do I make it out alive?

And if the alternative is being stuck here, wondering if every day is going to be my last, is it maybe smarter to let him do what he's going to do? Just to get it over with? Because the thing is, the longer I'm with him, the greater the chance of giving myself to him. If he had fucked me like an animal after going down on me, I would've let him and welcomed it. Hell, I would've fucked him back. And that simply cannot be.

When I think of it that way, it seems a lot easier to let him get this over with while I still have a little of my soul left. "I want to go home."

"I don't remember asking what you want." He finishes cleaning his plate, shooting me a filthy look. "Do me a favor and keep your bitching to yourself, okay?"

"Why should I?" He wants to play games? I can play games too. I fold my arms and arch an eyebrow, which means going against every self-preserving instinct I possess. This is not a man to screw around with, yet I'm doing it. "Here you are with all your threats and empty promises."

"Do you think they're empty?" The beginnings of a smile stir his lips, and like me, he folds his arms.

I don't back down. "So far, they have been. What's stopping you? Why not get it over with?"

"And what could you be referring to?" he counters, and something stirs low in my belly when he raises an eyebrow. "What is it? What are you in such a hurry for? For me to kill you like I said I would... or is it something else? Are you remembering how hard you came and wanting a little more?"

I am not going to shrink back this time. I will not look away when he hits me with that penetrative stare. "I want this to be over. You keep talking like you're going to end it. I wish you would."

"Is this reverse psychology? Do you think you'll stay alive by pretending you want to die?"

"I don't want to die," I assure him, shaking my head slowly. "But if this is living, I would rather it be over now."

His jaw tightens, and a million emotions pass over his handsome face—anger, confusion, dismay, and so many others—before he releases a soft growl that lifts the hair on the back of my neck. "Don't push me. You might end up getting your wish."

"Is that supposed to scare me?" I counter. "Because it doesn't. Not anymore."

"And why not?" He's breathing faster and harder as he places his palms against the table and rises from his chair.

"Because I know you don't want to kill me." I rise even though my leg screams its refusal. But I use it, grinding my teeth against it, turning all my helpless rage, fatigue, and despair into armor. "If you did, you would've done it by now. And you haven't contacted anybody about me... anybody who would care, though that's not a long list of people. So you're either keeping me because you don't know what to do with me or because you can't bring yourself to murder me. Which is it? What are you saving me for?"

He pins me in place with a hard, cold gaze, making my heart stutter. "Do not test me."

My body flushes with heat as his cologne envelops my senses. "That's not an answer."

He sweeps his arm over the table all at once, sending plates, forks, and glasses flying across the room. Then, he reaches out, taking my arm in a brutal grip that makes me grind my teeth and cry out in pain I can't contain. "Do you want to know what I'm saving you for?" He growls close to my face before turning me in place, forcing me to bend over the table thanks to the hand he presses against the center of my back.

An entire cacophony of conflicting emotions engulfs me like wildfire through dry brush. The fear, anger, and desire, one after another, surge through me too fast for me to hold onto. Panic unleashes in my mind and the dim but very real instinct that demands I fight.

But louder and stronger than that is the heat that bursts

to life at his touch, as his rough hands paw at my body and fondle my ass before he reaches around to cup my pussy. I bite down on my clenched fist, hoping to hold back a moan of sheer, helpless want.

"Is this enough of an answer for you?" He takes me by the hips and grinds against me, and I fight back another moan when I feel that impossibly large bulge rubbing against my ass crack. Something akin to joy erupts low in my belly when he starts tugging on my pants.

Until…

We both go still when tires crunch the leaves and sticks outside the cabin. Then, all at once, a million images run through my mind. This could be my salvation, or it could be the end of me. I shoot a panicked look over my shoulder to find Luca staring at the door, his eyes narrowed into dark, deadly slits like an animal that has sensed danger.

"You're so ready to die, Detective?" He pulls me upright, his gaze still trained on the door as he grips me tight. "This might be your lucky day."

16

LUCA

I should've known this was coming.

"Who could it be?" Emilia's frantic whisper echoes the question ringing out in my head. Did my father decide against waiting for me to come home? Or maybe it was Dante who ran out of patience. As far as I know, only the family knows this house's location.

"Don't move." I cross the cabin in a few long, quiet strides, stopping beside the front window so I can take a look at our visitor.

Our visitors, as it turns out. Three men dressed in shades of brown and dark green climb out of a black SUV and look around, sizing up their surroundings. Do they think they're going to blend in wearing those clothes? I don't recognize any of them, but that doesn't matter. I didn't know Emilia's assassin was sent by my father, either.

My heart jumps into my throat when one of the men reaches into the rear of the vehicle and withdraws a semi-automatic rifle, which he uses to shoot out my tires.

So much for subtlety.

"Luca!" Emilia's startled cry rings out, and I've made

my decision before my body starts to move. I could pull my gun from the safe, fire on them, and maybe even get a decent shot or two, but I'm out armed and outnumbered. And that would leave her defenseless.

I rush back to where she crouches beside the kitchen table, then flip it onto its side for us to take cover behind. "How many are there?" she asks before a bullet pierces the front door, and we both duck.

"Three. Semi-automatics."

"Then give me my fucking gun! Where did you hide it?"

That is the last thing I should do. "I can handle it. Go to the bedroom," I order, shoving her in that direction.

All she does is push back, digging in. "What do you think I'm going to do? Shoot you?"

Yes. That's exactly what I'm afraid of. And why wouldn't she to free herself? The front window explodes inward in a storm of shattered glass, and the front door looks more like Swiss cheese when I dare peer around the table.

"Come on!" she urges. "Give us a chance!"

Fuck it.

I turn toward the drawers beneath the kitchen counter. When I slide the bottom drawer open, Emilia gasps at the sight of the safe and its electronic keypad. I don't know whether she makes note of the code as I punch it in, and right now, I don't care. The bullets flying in all directions and breaking the cabin apart are more concerning.

"Don't make me regret this." I hand over the service weapon taken from her apartment bathroom, and something close to grim satisfaction twists her lips into a grin as she looks it over. "Remember. Anything happens to me, and they get their hands on you, you're fucked."

"No shooting you," she barks out. "I get the message."

A bullet hits the edge of the table, and we duck. That was too close. Then, just as suddenly as the gunfire erupted, everything goes silent. There is nothing but the blood rushing in my ears and Emilia's strangled gasps for air.

A voice then calls out, almost taunting, singsong. "Send her out, Santoro!" the voice implores. "We might even let you leave in one piece. Anything between us can be settled another day. Right now, all we want is her." She flinches, whimpering softly, and I remind myself she might be a detective, but she's still a young woman in way over her head. She's never played the game at this level before.

Then I recall the damage they've done to my car. How would I leave with my tires blown out? Easy. They don't expect me to leave.

That begs the question, whose guys are they? I doubt my father would allow anyone to open fire on the cabin knowing I'm inside, but then he could've bet on me being able to take care of myself. I wish I didn't have to question my father's motives, but that's the path I've set myself on.

All thanks to the woman beside me, who makes no announcement before she begins to army crawl across the floor, sliding on her stomach until she reaches the sofa. The window is blown out now, and glass covers the cushions. She tosses them aside and climbs onto the couch, peering over the sill before ducking her head again. She's either the ballsiest person I've ever met or entirely out of her mind on adrenaline that's pushed aside her pain in favor of survival.

She looks back at me, our eyes meeting from opposite sides of the room. Gone is the timid, trembling thing I saved from certain death. She wants blood.

That makes two of us.

I clear my throat before raising my voice. "And if I hand her over…" I call out, "… you go? That's it?"

"That's it!"

Again, Emilia peers over the windowsill. She lifts her free hand, opening and closing it like a duck's bill. They're talking it over. She then gives me a thumbs up.

I begin moving out from behind the table, watching her watch the men. "All right. I'll bring her out. Hold your fire, dammit." Vitali is not sending his best on these missions.

Emilia nods, holding a hand in the air and lowering it, signaling they've dropped their weapons.

She waves me over, and I crawl across the floor the way she did, careful to avoid the glass. I take her place, gripping her wrist when she moves toward the door. "I'll open it, but stay covered," she breathes out close to my ear. "I'll draw their fire. You take them out."

"Come on, Santoro!" I'm almost glad that arrogant prick called out when he did, or else I might have no choice but to kiss this brave woman. I release her, and she nods firmly before creeping over to the door, bent at the waist.

Her hand closes around the knob, and I take aim at the man positioned in front of the door. I'll drop him first since he would have the clearest shot at Emilia, and I don't doubt that will startle the other two into opening fire. I only hope she gets clear in time.

She'd better.

She draws a deep breath, then flings the door open, leaping back toward the sofa. I give them a split second to react before opening fire, taking down the center shooter with a single shot to the neck.

"Stay down!" I shout to Emilia before firing on the man closest to me, who manages to blow more holes in the wall before I hit his kneecap and then his abdomen. He goes down screaming, squeezing the trigger, and sending bullets spraying in all directions. Emilia shrieks at the sudden burst of splinters and couch stuffing filling the air as bullets tear through the wood plank walls and into the room. I move out from my cover and throw myself over her, and for one moment—no more than a heartbeat—I wonder if this is it.

The end.

What's left of the front door is kicked open from outside, and the third shooter bursts into the cabin. Before his vision can adjust to the change in light, I twist, take aim, and fire. His head snaps back, and he slides to the floor, a look of surprise still on his face while he paints the wood behind him a deep shade of red.

The rest of me remains still, my body shielding Emilia's. The air is full of smoke and the coppery tang of blood. The silence is deafening.

"Are you all right? Are you hit?" I push myself up on my knees, looking her over, running my hands over her body.

"I'm fine. Really, I'm fine." She works her way to her feet, and I do the same, both of us staring at the destruction. I look out the window to where the other two men lie face down, neither moving.

"We'll have to take their car." I take hold of her, forcing her to the bedroom while my mind races with questions of what this means and whether there could be others on their way. I can't risk her again. "Get your stuff. We need to move."

"We?" She yanks her arm free of my grasp once we're beside the bed, breathing hard, still coming down from the rush of victory the way I am. "Why is it we? Why didn't you just hand me over?"

The ticking of an invisible clock reverberates in my

skull. "Now is not the time," I insist. "Either you move
your ass, or I move it for you. They might have sent—"

Her eyes are wide. Unblinking, stopping me from
finishing my warning. "Then stop wasting time and tell
me," she growls out. "Why didn't you give me to them?"

I look down at her right hand and the gun still in her
grasp. "You tell me. Why didn't you blow me away? You
could still do it. Go ahead. The way is clear."

Her tongue moistens her lips while her wide eyes move
over my face. "I…"

"You can't, can you?" That's all it takes to make her
eyes dart away. She wants to hide from me. "Look at me,
Emilia. You can't hurt me any more than I can hurt you."

"I could," she whispers, and I'll give it to her. She
attempts to appear serious, tossing her head back and
snickering. "But I'd only end up screwing myself over.
We're in the middle of nowhere, remember?"

This stubborn, impossible woman fought alongside me
and showed more bravery than I've seen from men who
trained for years to guard my family. She was ready,
determined to take on those guys and whoever followed.

She offers no resistance when I take the gun from her
hand and place it on the table beside the bed. "I'll tell you
why I won't hand you over."

"What are you doing?" she asks, stiffening but doing
nothing to stop me from pulling her close and reveling in
the touch of her warm, ripe body against mine, reminding
myself she's alive and whole, and I am too. It's pointless to
pretend I didn't already crave her with every fiber of my
being long before she displayed her smarts and bravery.
Life is too short to deny something as fundamental as us
being together.

I sink my hands into her thick hair and tilt her face so
our mouths line up. Her short, quick breaths hit my face.

Her wide, blue eyes search mine. "What are you doing?" she asks again, this time in a weak whisper.

What I've wanted to do all this time. I claim Emilia's mouth, parting her lips to invade her with my tongue, to undo every last bit of resistance still keeping us apart. This time, she doesn't fight. She melts against me all at once, her hands sliding over my bare chest, nails scraping my skin. My body ignites with desire, sparking my adrenaline at her touch.

I release her long enough to peel the shirt away from my body and throw it to the floor. When our gazes crash, the fire behind hers has me on her in a heartbeat. She wraps her arms around my neck, pulling me down, kissing me as hard as I'm devouring her while we tumble together onto the bed.

There's no hint of pain as she works her way out of her yoga pants, fumbling and shaking. I help her before dropping my pants and pulling my boxer briefs to my knees. There's no time for taking it slow, exploring. This is sheer instinct, reminding ourselves we're alive. We won this battle.

She closes her legs around me as I guide myself into her, pressing forward, filling her tight heat in one sure, smooth stroke, making her back arch and her mouth fall open in abandon. "Oh…" That's all she manages before I cover her mouth again, pushing my tongue inside the way I thrust with my cock, taking her hard, rough, possessing her body while giving her mine.

I bite her bottom lip, and she moans at the connection. It's never been like this. I take. I don't give. But there's no other name for what's happening as she meets me stroke for stroke, jerking her hips, pulling me deeper with her legs. Clawing at my back, my scalp, even sinking her teeth into my shoulder, when a deep stroke drives her into the mattress and pushes the metal bed frame against the wall. She needs this as much as I do, this coming together, this give-and-take.

Mine. Mine. The word echoes in my head each time our bodies slam together. Every stroke takes me closer to the inevitable, cementing our bond. I pour myself into her, marking her skin with my kiss, bruising her lips, sucking the tender skin of her throat between my teeth until she writhes and moans my name. "Luca… Luca…"

"Yes." I lift my head to gaze down at her. I'm lost in her as she is in me. Her eyes are hazy, her face flushed, and her lips swollen. "Say my name. *Say it*," I grit out.

"Luca." It pours from her lips like warm honey, and the sound unlocks something deeper, surer, and primal.

This is my woman.

And somewhere along the line, I became her man.

She arches again before her muscles clench tight around my dick. I can't hold on any longer. Not when her pussy is determined to milk me dry. "Luca! I'm… I'm…"

I take a single moment to indulge in the sensation of her muscles fluttering around me before sinking deep, burying myself to the hilt, and bathing her with my seed.

She's mine. The thought is so abrupt that it steals my breath. It's taken root. We are meant to be together.

Once I push up on my forearms to look down at her, I see the same certainty in her half-closed eyes. "You do understand I would never let that happen if I wasn't on birth control," she whispers, and it amazes me how, even now, she has to cling to a sense of control. Then her eyes open wider. This time, there's no shame behind them when she speaks. "Now what?"

That one is easy. "Now, we get the hell out of here."

"Where?"

That's the thing. I have no idea. "We'll figure it out."

Not five minutes pass before we're on our way outside, both of us still armed in case a second wave arrives. "We need the keys," I announce, checking the body still slumped against the front door.

She heads out, going to the man who almost blew us both away when he shot up the cabin as he was dying. I'm standing in the doorway as she rolls him onto his back.

I see the pistol before she does. "Emilia!"

A shot rings out, and she gasps, staggering backward. The shooter takes aim, barely lifting his head from the ground.

Only to fall back when I pump a bullet into his skull.

"*Emilia.* Oh, fuck." I drop to one knee beside her, where the right sleeve of her sweater has gone dark red. She presses a hand against the wound, but blood flows from between her fingers.

"Stay still. Try to stay calm." I'm babbling without thinking, fumbling with my belt, pulling it free, and wrapping it around her upper arm before cinching as tight as I can. "It looks like it went through," I tell her as she fights to control her breathing, whimpering and groaning when I pull the belt tighter. The sound is a knife in my chest, twisting and turning, shredding what's left of my heart.

"So stupid," she whispers, shaking her head. "I should know better. Why don't I know better?"

"Don't worry about it." Because in the end, I should've protected her.

She's mine.

She always has been.

I should have seen this coming.

As it turns out, he had the keys. I pull them free before pulling her to her feet. "Let's go."

"Where?" she asks for a second time while I try to

ignore the pool of blood she left behind. I practically have to lift her into the SUV, and her plea is weak, "I need help."

"And I'll get it for you," I vow before closing the door.

Even if it means having to beg, I'll get it for her.

17

EMILIA

Sounds and images flow together until I don't know what's real and what's the product of my weakening grip on consciousness. I can barely keep my eyes open as Luca flies away from the cabin, taking the rough terrain at a hair-raising speed and making us bounce in our seats. I don't have the strength to tell him to be careful. I'm losing too much blood. Or I did. It appears to have slowed when I get up the courage to look down at the bloody mess my arm has become.

"Luca..." I whisper, and even that single word takes effort.

"Save your strength," he barks out, steering with one blood-covered hand while handling his phone with the other. He needs to keep his attention on the road while driving this fast, but I can't make my mouth form the warning.

My eyes slowly close, and I welcome the darkness. There's no pain in the dark. No fear.

"Listen to me!" My eyes open, though I don't think he

was speaking to me. There's someone on the phone, someone he's shouting at while we career down a two-lane mountain road. I slept through the drive up here, so it's not only the dizzy, woozy feeling in my head that leaves me confused. I don't even know how far we are from home.

"She needs help, and she needs it now!" he shouts. "No, I can't take her to a fucking hospital... what's wrong with you? You know damn well what would happen."

A hospital.

My salvation.

But he wouldn't be able to stay with me, would he? My heart sinks at the thought of him leaving me there, alone. He would have to go. He's still my kidnapper.

I won't tell them. *I won't tell anybody.* The thought surprises me, but it feels right. I would let Luca go. I would pretend not to know who left me at the hospital. I could fake shock, something, whatever it took to keep him out of it. Keep him safe.

He could have handed me over to those men at the cabin. He could've killed me so many times. Instead, he's fighting with whoever is on the other side of the phone, which I'm guessing is someone from his family.

He's fighting for me.

"I think the bleeding has slowed down." I open my eyes long enough to see we're taking an on-ramp onto a highway—Route 80—heading east, going home. "But it will still be a couple hours. Is there any way we can meet between here and there? Yes, with the doctor, goddammit! What do you think? How the fuck did Vitali know about the safe house?"

He's frantic, losing his grip. I want to tell him to calm down and there's nothing to freak out about. I'm actually feeling kind of good now. The pain has subsided a little, and a warm, comfortable feeling replaces it, like being wrapped in thick blankets on a cold day.

I would tell him all those things, only I can't get up the strength to speak. It's so much easier to let the darkness enfold me and pull me down deep.

―――――

IT'S QUIET.

My eyes open slowly, and the first thing I notice is the soft pillows behind my head. I'm lying on my back under a thick, down comforter. There's a little table to my left where bottled water and tissues sit, and beyond that is a window where thin light trickles in between the closed slats of the blinds. Morning or dusk? I can't tell. But I'm comfortable.

It's a good start.

Then, I remember everything all at once, the shooting, so vivid in my memory that I can hear the bullets tearing through the wood around us. I can smell the smoke in the blood.

My blood.

I look down at my right arm, surprised to find my sweater replaced by a white, sleeveless nightgown. Large gauze pads cover me from my shoulder to halfway to my elbow. I move a little and don't feel any pain, noting they must've given me something for it.

But who are they?

And where am I?

"You're awake."

My startled gasp rings out as I turn my head to find a stranger sitting in an armchair to the right of my bed. Even if he didn't look so much like his son, I would recognize him on sight. "Mr. Santoro," I croak, noting his distinctive silver hair and a nose permanently flattened after being broken one too many times. My throat is so dry like I haven't had anything to drink in days.

"Miss Washington." His voice is deep, gravelly. "Or should I say, Detective Washington?"

The blood freezes in my veins. He must know how frightening this is. No doubt he's taking a little bit of pleasure in it. "I didn't think you knew that," I whisper.

"I know a lot of things now." He folds his thick hands in his lap, and I have to deliberately stop myself from wondering how many lives those hands have snuffed out. "You see, my son had no choice but to confess everything if there was any chance of allowing you in my home."

His home? *He took me to his father's compound?* How could he do that? Why would he do it? "He could've left me at a hospital," I whisper more to myself than to him.

The lines at the corners of his dark eyes deepen, and he even chuckles. "Yes, I told him the same thing. How interesting to find we think along the same lines, you and I."

Here's hoping that's where the similarities end. I may have made the mistake of getting too close to his son, but the father is another matter. I can barely keep my thoughts together under the weight of his judgmental gaze. "Where is he?"

His thin, forced humor dies, replaced by stony refusal. "That's nothing for you to worry about."

"But he's all right?" My heart pounds as I search his face, desperate for confirmation that Luca hasn't been punished for rescuing me.

This is not a man who allows his true reactions to show. He can't afford it. Nobody in a position of power can. Yet his eyes fly open wide in the split second before he reins himself in. "And you care… why?"

"Because I do. He tried so hard to help me when I was injured. He defended me." It sounds silly now that I've said it out loud, but I'm not going to take it back. It's a much safer admission than the one that would directly answer his question.

I'm reasonably sure I fell for Luca somewhere along the way.

He scoffs before his mouth tightens into a smirk that makes him look painfully similar to his son. "All in all, he's fine," he reports, answering my original question. "Not as all right as he would have been had you never darkened his doorstep, of course. It's been a relief for his mother to have him home these past few days."

"Couple of days?" I try to lift my head, but the room starts spinning.

"Relax," he urges in a deceptively soft voice. "No need to worry. Yes, you've been asleep all this time. My wife was generous enough to help clean you up and even gave you one of her nightgowns. You lost a great deal of blood, but our family doctor got you stitched up and thinks you'll be just fine. Although, I hate to say it…"

My heart forgets to beat for a second. "What?"

"It looks like you'll be on desk duty from now on, Detective. He said there's a good chance of nerve damage, and that's your dominant hand. Sorry about that." The twitching of his lips conveys a very different sentiment.

He's not sorry, and we both know it. He is barely containing his hatred, his loathing, digging the knife in at precisely the place where he knows it will cause the most damage. A desk cop? No fucking way. I didn't work as hard as I have to sit behind a desk for the rest of my life, developing carpal tunnel, while men and women without half my dedication are out there living my destiny. The idea turns my stomach and sends bitterness racing through my veins.

I don't trust a word out of this man's mouth. He's only trying to scare me. It's Luca I trust. As bizarre as the idea is, as surprised as I am to have it, it feels true. Nobody can pretend to be as panicked as he was when I was shot. That was genuine. I take the memory, hold it close to my heart, and hope I'm not wrong. "I would like to see him," I whisper. "Please. Can I speak to Luca?"

Rocco's head snaps back before his shrewd eyes go narrow. "I told you he gave you up as a cop, and you still want to see him?"

He's trying way too hard to make me hate his son. I need to remember this is a shrewd, calculating man who's a pro at twisting people up. It would be a mistake to take everything he says as truth. "You didn't give him a choice, and I still want him to know I'm okay."

He snorts in disbelief. "I'll make sure he's aware."

All this is doing is making me more determined to see Luca. There's got to be a reason his father is dead set on keeping us apart. He has to know there's nothing I can do to hurt his family while lying in a bed and unable to lift my head off the pillow without practically passing out. "I'm sure he wants to see me too."

"And you care what my son wants… why?" he demands, his tone leaving a wake of goose bumps on my skin. "He kidnapped you after stalking you for days. Don't tell me you've developed a soft spot." I wish my face wouldn't heat up the way it is at his insinuation and the nastiness behind it. "I think you've done enough speaking to Luca," he continues. "The fact is, my son has lost sight of his priorities. Whether or not that's your fault is a matter of opinion, but I am of the opinion you are to blame. What do I do about that?" He purses his lips like he's actually pondering the question.

Let me go. Yeah, right. Like that would happen. He's a cold-blooded murderer. This heartless bastard has destroyed so many lives through his violence, corruption, and the way he and the men who worked for his father before him exploited countless people and their addictions. Human life is cheap to them.

And why the hell would Luca be any different? Have I been kidding myself? It's easy to do that when you're in a bubble, and all you can focus on is getting through one hour at a time.

"Maybe I've given you too much to think about in your weakened state." He stands, grunting a little like he's starting to feel his sixty-five years. "Suffice it to say, Luca is home where he belongs, and he'll understand and follow along with whatever it is I decide to do with you. Finally getting some rest has realigned his priorities. Maybe I should thank you for getting shot," he offers with a smirk. "You brought him back to us. Thank you for that, Detective Washington."

Hot, furious tears fill my eyes as I stare at his retreating form. "Don't get any ideas," he adds on his way out. "You're being watched. I might have taken you in for the sake of getting my son back, but that's where the hospitality ends. Behave yourself, and I might make it quick for you."

"Why not get it over with now?" I ask before he's closed the door between us.

He pauses, then lifts a shoulder. "You might still be valuable."

Maybe I should thank Rocco for reminding me of just who and what I got myself involved with. It would probably do me no good now that he's clearly bent on killing me. Still, at least I could die without laboring under the illusion that anyone in this violent, heartless world could truly care about anyone or anything but their family business. Knowing all that, I still can't help but long for Luca.

18

LUCA

I now know how a caged tiger feels.

I've never considered the house my father built for me within the walls of the family compound to be anything less than a haven. After a long meeting or a family dinner, there was nothing like escaping here to decompress. It's no bigger than the cabin where I stayed with Emilia, but it's much more comfortable.

At least, it usually feels that way. Now it's a gilded cage, one I pace helplessly while God only fucking knows what goes on at the house. One of the conditions of Papa taking in Emilia and making sure she received treatment, I'm stuck here until he decides it's safe to let me out. There are armed men at my front door, working in shifts.

Never did I think my own father would hold me hostage.

Never did I think I would give him any reason to.

But I couldn't have expected her to walk into my life.

Has she walked out of it? I made him swear. I begged him to vow he wouldn't hurt her. My mother was there, so she heard him promise. If nothing else, he'll keep a promise he made in front of her.

I need to believe he will.

Otherwise, what was this all for?

Two days.

Two days without her, without knowing anything other than the fact that she was alive and still unconscious when I left her up at the house. Dr. Graham has been with the family since before I was born. I have no doubt he would do everything necessary to take care of her. What worries me is what happened after he left. I imagine Dante whispering in Papa's ear, insisting all outsiders are threats.

An animal growl stirs in my chest, and I kick the coffee table in passing, sending it sliding across the floor. It does nothing to ease the pressure threatening to tear me apart. I'm helpless, a little better than a fucking baby, with no say in anything happening around me. And all because I met her.

If two days spent in captivity have done nothing else, they've given me perspective. I've had to come to terms with a lot of shit I've wasted time denying. I'm finished pretending not to know why I went to the trouble I went to for her sake. I know damn well it's because I fell for her the moment I set eyes on her at the club. If I hadn't, none of this would be happening. She would be nothing more than a dim memory at this moment.

But no, I lost control of the situation before I knew there was one. I never had a chance against her.

And while I have no idea what the future will look like, considering we are the least likely pair imaginable, I am not going to face it without her. Deep down, I know she feels the same way. She might not be ready to admit it to herself yet, but some things can't be denied forever. She's mine, plain and simple. And I have gone against everything I thought mattered for her sake.

There are voices outside the front door. Familiar ones. I brace myself, pushing the sleeves of my sweatshirt up to my elbows. Considering this is the first visit I've received since I was escorted here, I figure it must be important.

Dante steps through the door first because, of course, he does. Why would he waste an opportunity to look like a big man and be the first to glare at me in disappointment? "Going casual, I see," he remarks, eyeing my hoodie and sweatpants, clearly comparing them to his own bespoke suit.

I don't bother concealing my irritation. "It's the funniest thing. My schedule has been wide open the past couple of days, so I've been leaning more toward comfort." He simply rolls his eyes and steps aside for Papa to enter after his brief conversation with my guard.

The fact that he barely glances at me confirms he's not feeling much more generous than he did on my arrival. "She's awake. Thought you'd want to know," Papa says in a detached voice.

His words stir up relief I can't contain. "She's okay? You've seen her?"

The two of them exchange a look that's heavy with meaning. It sets my teeth on edge until I can't help but blurt out, "Would you stop acting as though she's a deadly weapon? There is nothing wrong with me being concerned about her."

"*Obsessed* with her," Dante mutters.

"Stand down," Papa advises with a sigh, staring down at the fists clenched at my sides until I loosen them. "I'm not going to have you two bickering and throwing punches. That's not what we're here for."

"Then what are you here for?" I ask, irritation coating

my words as I look back and forth between them. "For two days, you've ignored me, and now you show up unannounced."

"Are you sure there's nothing you want to tell us?" Dante asks in a deceptively soft voice. Instantly, my hackles rise. What is he driving at?

"You'll have to elaborate," I fire back. "What are you referring to?"

"Son." Dad heaves a sigh, lowering his brow like a bull ready to charge. "Enough bullshit. We know who she is. One of our guys in the NYPD got word of a detective who went missing from her apartment out in Brooklyn. We got our hands on the address. It doesn't take a rocket scientist to put everything together."

I would swear every drop of blood in my veins has turned to solid ice. Just when I think they can't surprise me, they drop a bomb on my head. They've known who she is and expect me to believe she's still safe?

It was inevitable, wasn't it? That's what I have to tell myself as I absorb this without any major reaction. Call me a stubborn prick, but I'm not going to let them know they startled me. "And you're still going to tell me she's alive and well?"

"You aren't surprised?" Papa asks, incredulous, while Dante sputters.

"It was bound to happen. With all of your inside connections?" I shrug blithely and don't bother hiding my satisfaction when Dante's tanned face goes red. What did he expect? That I'd collapse in tears?

"You knew all along, didn't you?" he demands. "You stalked and kidnapped a fucking detective assigned to taking down the *famiglia.*"

"And the Vitali," I add. "She would've gotten around to them too."

"At a time like this, you make jokes?" Dad shouts, his voice loud enough to make both of us flinch. No, there's nothing funny about this, but I need to get my satisfaction where I can, and Dante's indignation is very satisfying.

"Clearly, she was unsuccessful," I remind them. "So no, I don't see the point in holding that against her now. She has not done anything to get in our way."

"Like hell, she hasn't," Dante growls out. "Or have you forgotten the Vitali are determined to get their fucking hands on her? And here you are, protecting her, shielding her, killing for her. Pouring gasoline on the fire. She doesn't have to arrest any of us to be successful in taking us down. You've practically handed us to her on a silver platter."

I hear what he's saying, but it means nothing. "That's not true. We were already going to war with Vitali, and that's not on us. Allesandro is a fucking psychopath. He only needed…" My voice quits on me when my brain catches up with my mouth and reveals what a smacked ass I am.

"Go ahead," Dante urges in a voice that brings to mind a snake's hiss. "Finish your thought."

He only needed an excuse. "He would've found some other reason to accelerate things," I insist.

"Who are you trying to convince?" Dante asks, wearing a sickening smirk. "Us or yourself?"

"Go to hell." I snarl.

"Listen to yourself," Papa urges. "You would tell your own brother to go to hell over some little bitch cop?"

Something caustic, like acid, rises in my chest and comes dangerously close to pouring from my mouth in the form of words I couldn't take back. I won't disrespect my father that way, but he's taking me damn close to the point where I can't be held accountable for my actions.

"Don't tell me you're in love with her," Dante taunts,

snickering, and all I can do is stare at the floor and remind myself how it would break our mother's heart if I snapped his neck. "Of all the ways you could fuck up."

"Enough." It's rare for Papa to get sharp with his eldest son, the golden child, and watching Dante's face fall is gratifying. "Remember, at the end of the day, we are all we have. It's bad enough that somebody got in the way. We don't need to push each other farther away and make her job easier. Got it?"

"I'm telling you, it's not like that now." I wish I could get it through his head. Both of them. Why can't they take my word for it?

Papa looks skeptical, putting it mildly. "And what makes you think that? Have the two of you discussed this?"

"We didn't exactly get the chance."

He cups the back of my neck with his hand. A gesture as familiar to me as the sound of his voice. It used to comfort me. "I'll give her one bit of credit. I told her you ratted her out to us, thinking she'd turn on you and show her true colors. She didn't."

The idea that he's fucked with her head makes my blood boil, but my pride in Emilia cools me off. "See?" I ask, vindicated. Or so I think.

His grip tightens until I grind my teeth. "How do you know she doesn't intend to march into that station just as soon as she gets up her strength and tell her boss and anybody else who'll listen all about our operation?"

"For one thing, she knows nothing about it. I haven't told her shit, and that's the truth. I haven't completely gone off the deep end," I add, glaring at my brother.

"It's only a matter of time," he insists. "It's obvious she's already broken you down. All she had to do next was start asking the right questions."

She wouldn't have done that. *But how do you know?*

I hate that question.

I hate the fact that the idea is in my head at all.

I hate that I don't remember exactly when I became so sure of her.

Maybe it was when she could've taken me out with her service pistol but didn't. Something changed back there at the cabin. I know I'll never be able to make them understand simply by explaining it, especially since I can't explain it to myself.

"Papa." It's a last-ditch effort, and I'm not exactly proud of myself, but I'm starting to understand there are people worth losing your pride over. "Please. Isn't it enough that I'm telling you I believe in her? Can you trust my judgment?"

"No, I can't. That's the sad part." My father shakes his head and looks more disappointed than I remember seeing him in a long time. "This might as well be Frankie all over again, son."

"This is nothing like that. I'm telling you," I defend and, what the hell? I might as well spell it out for him. "I care about her."

"Do you honestly think she feels the same way about you?" Dante snorts before looking to our father for backup, but Papa remains ominously quiet.

"I don't know," I admit, which is not exactly easy. "But I want to find out. At least give me that chance."

Dante throws his hands into the air. "And what if she doesn't? What then? What's that going to change?"

That's the thing. I can't bring myself to imagine a world in which Emilia doesn't care about me. I'm sure it's possible, but something inside won't let me entertain the thought. "I'll handle it."

"How would you do that?" Papa demands. "Because if what you've done so far is your idea of handling things, it would appear we have very different definitions."

"Trust me." I look at both of them, and there's never been a point in my life when I've been so completely at their mercy, not even for my own sake, but for hers. For the first time, there's someone who matters to me more than my blood. More than myself.

Dante clears his throat, barely bothering to conceal a gleeful smirk. "We better get moving," he tells Papa. "We have that meeting."

"Oh, yes…" He pauses, drawing out the suspense. "A meeting with the Vitali representatives."

"Are you serious?" The idea sets off every red flag imaginable in my head. "You can't go to something like that without me. At least tell me you're taking Cesco with you." Francesco is, without a doubt, the family's most ruthless and devoted soldier. There aren't many people I trust more.

"It's all remote," Dante explains with a sigh. "No way are we going into the same room with any of those assholes. But thank you so much for your advice."

"We're trying to come to a peaceful resolution," Papa explains before I can tell my brother to get fucked. "At the end of the day, I've always been against getting into a war with Vitali. You kids today, you've never seen what a real war can do. It's all numbers, abstract bullshit. I've seen it with my own eyes. I've lost friends. It's too expensive and messy."

And you've taken us closer to it than we were before. He doesn't have to say it out loud. I hear it. I feel it. And I know he's right.

Would I change anything if I had the chance? No. That's what makes me sure what I feel for Emilia is real. I wouldn't change a thing.

Dante shakes his head with a scowl, muttering to himself on his way out the door. Papa lets him go, meeting my gaze once we're alone. "I've been too indulgent with you." There's regret in his voice, in his eyes. "I take a lot of this on my shoulders. You've always been your mother's favorite. There's never been a secret about that. And you know I would do anything to make her happy. But I let you get away with too much, and this is where it's gotten me."

"Papa." I would never say this in front of Dante, not if my life depended on it. "Papa, I know how you feel, and I understand. But it can't be helped. I care too much about her. She… she belongs to me."

I don't think I could've hurt him more profoundly if I'd hit him. He rocks back on his heels, and his throat works like there's a lump in it. He opens his mouth, prepared to speak, then decides against it, shaking his head before turning toward the door.

"I need to know if she's all right. Please." I sound like a junkie begging for a fix, and maybe that's who I am. That's how far I've fallen.

My father sighs before pulling his phone from his pocket and taps the screen a few times. He holds it up for me to see the video feed.

There she is, and I release a deep breath, closing my eyes to absorb the relief before studying the image. She's lying in bed, eyes closed, breathing deeply and evenly. "She's asleep," he so helpfully points out. "Safe and sound. And she'll stay safe and sound… for as long as it serves me."

"At least let me be there for the meeting." Because I can't bear the thought of her fate being decided without either of us being present. "I won't say a word, I'll sit off-camera, only—"

"That, I can't do." He puts the phone away, robbing

me of the sight of Emilia's sleeping body. "I want you to take a little time to remind yourself what this family means to you and what you mean to us."

Even if he wasn't in such a hurry to get to his meeting, I know there would be no making him see that the minute I met her, my life stopped being about me, my responsibilities, and my family.

If it comes down to it and I have to make a choice, I know, without a doubt, I would choose her.

19

EMILIA

I'm going crazy.

I've counted all five hundred and forty-two flowers on the wallpaper, I don't know how many times. But it was better than wasting precious energy trying to escape. The doors were deadlocked, the windows sealed shut.

This place is more secure than Fort Knox.

I'm free to go where I want and do what I want so long as it never takes me out of this room or the bathroom. A lavish bathroom whose door is always locked from the outside the way the bedroom door is, but at least I have privacy. There are no cameras in there that I'm aware of. There's only one mounted near the ceiling directly across from the foot of my double bed. I can't imagine they installed it just for my sake, but who knows? I was out cold. They probably could have marched an entire brass band through the room, and I never would've known.

At this point, it's easier to sleep than it is to be awake. At least when I'm asleep, I feel safe. I can dream. My subconscious can take me away to a world where things make sense, questions are answered, and I don't spend every second wondering when somebody will burst into this room and drag me out by my hair to do whatever it is they decide to do to me.

It's unsettling having no idea of the time. How long has it been since Rocco Santoro introduced himself to me? Actually, he didn't even do that. He knew I'd know who he was right away. The smug prick.

I see the apple doesn't fall too far from the tree.

Where is Luca? Is he ever going to come for me? If he doesn't, will it be because he decided not to, or they wouldn't let him? We're in a huge mess, putting it mildly. I would at least like to talk it over with him to see how he feels and what he's actually thinking.

I need to know I'm not in this alone, that I didn't make the stupid mistake of getting too close to him, caring too much, and trusting too much. I don't know when that shift occurred, and I've had plenty of time to think it over.

It feels like an eternity has passed since Rocco was here. All I know is it's gotten dark since then, then light again. The next morning? It must be.

I can't believe how much I want to believe in him. I can't believe how many times I've told myself he wouldn't betray me when that is precisely what he would do if he were smart. I am the last person he needs in his life, just like he's the last person I need, so why doesn't it feel that way? Why am I still hoping as I hobble across the room, awkwardly placing myself back in bed after washing up at the sink? There's no getting in the shower with these bandages unless I have a way to wrap them and keep them dry. I couldn't handle an infection weakening me further when I don't know if I can trust anybody under this roof.

I've decided to close my eyes and try to fall back to sleep, where I can at least be happy for a little while when a soft knock at the bedroom door makes my heart seize with fear. The lock clicks, and I hold my breath, wishing there was somewhere I could hide, telling myself not to reveal my fear to whoever is about to step through the door.

It's not Rocco, and it's not Luca, either. It's someone whose face I've seen only in photos, and even then, there aren't many available. Rocco tends to keep her away from the public eye.

"Hi," the girl whispers. Her thick, shoulder-length black curls bounce a little when she walks, carrying a tray with food that smells good enough to make my eyes water in gratitude. Her brilliant smile and wide, sparkling dark eyes make me stare in wonder. No wonder Rocco is so cautious with her. She's a ravishing beauty with sensuous features, but the sweetness that seems to radiate from her strikes me as reason enough to protect her.

"I'm Guilia," she announces brightly. "And you're Emilia, right?"

I'm taken off guard by her friendliness. "Right." What do I know about Guilia? Not much. She's younger than Rocco's sons, closer to my age than theirs. He treasures her the way he does his wife, the way so many of the men from these old Italian families do. They have no problem killing each other in cold blood, but their women? They venerate them. It's the strangest juxtaposition.

Guilia sets the tray on the bed, balancing it across my thighs. I should be wary of her, but something about her radiates innocence like she shouldn't be the daughter of a mob boss but is. "I asked if they would let me bring this up. Papa didn't like the idea, but Mama said I should. She said you could probably use a smile."

"She's right," I confess, smiling back at her. I wonder how she's managed to maintain her sweetness in a cruel, violent world like the one she was raised in.

"There's something else." She shoots a furtive look toward the camera before reaching into the pocket of her oversized cardigan and withdrawing a folded piece of paper. The sight of it makes my heart skip a beat. I'm hungrier for word from Luca than I've ever been for food, and instinct tells me that's what his sister has brought.

I take the paper in my trembling hand and unfold it while Guilia looks away like she's giving me privacy. Emotion rises in my chest at the sight of a hastily scribbled message.

Don't worry. I'm coming for you.

"He gave it to Mama," Guilia murmurs. "And she asked me to bring it to you."

"Thank you." I tuck the note under my blanket since I don't want Rocco to find me obsessing over it while he's spying on me.

He's thinking of me. He wants me not to worry. He's coming for me.

I don't know when, but I believe him, and that belief strengthens me.

"Are you thirsty?" She pulls out a bottle of water from the other pocket of her long cardigan. "I didn't want it to fall off the tray and knock everything else off with it," she explains with an awkward little laugh. "How are you feeling?"

Something about this girl and her openness is refreshing, almost disarming. I don't know how to react to her. "Tired," I murmur, eyeing the covered plate on the tray.

"You're probably starving. I'm sorry. Please, eat." She lifts the lid with a flourish, revealing a stack of French toast, bacon, and sausage. There's also a small bowl of berries and a tiny pitcher of syrup. I've stayed in hotels with a less impressive breakfast spread.

It isn't easy to speak with saliva flooding my mouth. "Thank you so much. I was starting to think everybody forgot about me."

It was an innocent comment, and it was the truth, but Guilia's dark eyes go wide anyway. "Oh, trust me. Nobody's forgotten about you. You're all anybody can talk about around here."

Now, I'm hungry for something beyond food, but that doesn't stop me from digging in with abandon. This is a far cry from the shitty pancakes Luca made. "I've caused a lot of trouble, haven't I?" I ask with my mouth full.

"You and Luca! You can't take all the blame."

I can tell there's something she wants to ask. She keeps opening her mouth, sucking in a breath like she's prepared to speak, then her mouth snaps shut, and she looks down at her folded hands. I wonder if she has a lot of friends, and if it's possible to have a normal social life when you're from a family like this. What would it be like, always guarded, constantly aware of the danger that could lurk around every corner? Because surely, she must know. There's no way she grew up here, among these men, without knowing what they do.

"How is he?" I whisper. It's a big risk, but she seems sympathetic. She might be my only shot at hearing anything about Luca.

She chews her lip, frowning. "I'd get in trouble for telling you."

"I do not want you to get in trouble," I assure her right away. "You can't tell me anything, and I get it. Just… is he okay?"

She starts bouncing up and down on the balls of her feet. "I really shouldn't, but I want to…" She throws her hands into the air with a sigh. "Papa's making him stay in

his house. There's somebody at the door day and night, so
he can't leave."

Somehow, in all the scenarios I have imagined while
lying here alone, that one never entered my mind. "Why?"
I whisper, forgetting the food as I ponder this.

"Promise you won't tell?" she asks, and I trace an X
over my heart. "Okay. I wasn't supposed to be listening,
but I heard Luca say he would stay there and stay away
from you so long as Papa promised to help you. You
must've bled a ton, and Luca was out of his mind. I have
never seen him like that, and it made me cry. It made
Mama cry too. I thought he was going to start throwing
things around, he was that upset."

"Over me?" I can't picture it, but damn if this doesn't
make me think this is real between us.

"Yeah, over you. He promised he would do whatever
Papa wants, but you had to be safe first." She offers a tiny
shrug. "I'm sorry, but it's kind of romantic. Like he was
ready to hurt somebody if they got in his way. I know I'm
not supposed to know about any of this, and I know for
sure Papa would kill me if he knew I told you, but I can't
help how I feel about it."

"Thank you for telling me," I whisper, reeling, almost
dumbstruck, before something occurs to me. I look up at
the camera, then at her. "I'm being watched," I whisper,
horrified.

She waves it off. "Don't worry about it. There's no
audio."

I'm starting to wonder who got the brains in this family
because Guilia is pleasantly surprising me. "You are a very
observant person, aren't you?"

"I pay attention," she admits with a grin. "And now I
better go. Are you gonna be okay? Do you need anything
else right now?"

He was violently upset. He's being kept from me but slipped a note to his mother to bring up here. He deserves to hear from me. "Do you have a pen?"

Her eyes twinkle as she reaches into her pocket once again. "I thought you would want to write him back. This is so romantic, I'm going to scream."

"Don't do that," I murmur with a grin, taking the pen and jotting down a note for Luca across a paper napkin. What to say? There isn't enough room for everything I'm carrying in my heart. I settle for keeping it short and sweet.

I'm here, waiting and safe. Please be careful.

I stop myself before I can write anything stupid like *I love you*, folding up the napkin instead and handing it to Guilia. "Thank you, Guilia. It's so nice to meet you."

She tucks the note in her pocket along with the pen. Her eyes still twinkle like she's having the time of her life. "Same here. I'll try to come back later with lunch and, you know, whatever else needs to be delivered." Then she's gone, and somehow, the room seems a little dimmer without her in it.

I wish he'd had the chance to say more than those two short sentences, mainly because I don't know how to feel about what I just learned and would appreciate an explanation. He went against his father, his family. He essentially made himself a prisoner on the grounds so long as it meant me getting the help I needed. The way Guilia described it, he was on the brink of losing his grip completely and all because of me.

I figured he had to be obsessed with me. Why else would he have gone to the lengths he did otherwise? Sneaking around my apartment, even murdering for my sake.

But standing up to his father? If I woke up to find ten

million dollars in my checking account, I couldn't be more stunned. I don't know how to feel or what to think.

I don't know who I am anymore. All thanks to a mafia man who, at this moment, is locked in his own home, kept away from me.

Away from his family.

Because of me.

I close my eyes, covering them with one trembling hand in hopes of hiding my tears from whoever is watching me. I refuse to give them the satisfaction.

20

LUCA

There is no fucking way I'm spending another minute in this house.

I check my phone, reviewing the latest text from my cousin, Niccolo. Why the hell it took me so long to consider texting him, I have no idea. I've always considered him the brother I should have had. We have more in common, and we've gotten along better because we understand each other in the way Dante and I never will.

We're both second sons, neither of us expected to sit at the head of anything. To make it worse for him, he's the second son of a second son, Papa's brother, Tomasso, who died a few years back. Once Papa absorbed all of the businesses his brother managed, Niccolo came to work for us.

Niccolo: *I'll be down as soon as the meeting ends. Wrapping up.*

He was invited to attend a meeting I was forbidden to attend. I have devoted my life to learning our business, understanding the connections we have to other families—

friend and foe alike—learning the intricacies of the diplomacy needed to avoid war, and nurturing long alliances.

I've been left behind because I refuse to back down and sacrifice the one thing that has ever made me question my loyalty. I'm going to find a way for us to be together.

End of story.

They'll have to get used to it.

Niccolo: *On my way.*

He'll keep this between us. We've covered for each other more than once, though it was never anything with stakes as high as they are now. Has anything ever been? Incredible, the way Emilia has realigned my priorities and set everything in order.

Right now, my priority lies with seeing and touching her. A simple image on my father's phone isn't enough. He should know better than to think I'd be satisfied with that. I'm too much like him to be anything but demanding.

Voices ring out on the other side of my front door, right on schedule. "Go ahead, grab some grub." Niccolo's approach doesn't give off any hint that he's hiding something.

"I'm supposed to be here for another two hours." I don't know which of the guys is on guard right now, but he doesn't seem to be one of the brighter ones. They don't have to be—strong and ruthless gets the job done.

"Go ahead. I already ate, and my uncle wants everyone to stay close, so I'm not going anywhere."

Another minute passes before the door swings open. The sight of Niccolo's swarthy face is a relief. "Thanks. You're a lifesaver. None of the regular guards would've let me out."

"It's nothing." He shrugs it off as I join him outside and lock the door. There's a light on, and I left the television tuned to football. If I'm still up at the house when my next guard shows up, they'll think I'm watching the game in peace. They know better than to check in with me unless they feel like hearing what I think about being locked up, whether it was my idea or not.

My quick, anxious breaths leave a fog around my head as we make our way along the eastern side of the main house. Anxious for Emilia, not for myself. There's one lesson we boys learned a long time ago with no help from our fathers—how to sneak in and out unnoticed.

When I was a kid, the old men used to tell stories of how bootleg liquor was run through this very property, delivered from Canada, stored here, then shipped out across New York using tunnels running underground to keep outsiders unaware of the activity. In the decades since, my family has twice used the tunnels for the sake of safety, bundling the women and children through them when shit hit the fan.

We reach a door carved into the earth, sitting just inside the thick wall separating us from the rest of the world. There's an iron gate here, half-hidden by overgrown shrubs. You'd have to know what you're looking for to notice it, just like you'd have to know the door exists to find it covered in dead branches and weeds.

"What's the temperature like in the house?" I ask as I crouch, searching for the handle while my cousin keeps a lookout.

He grunts, almost like he's in pain. "Pretty hot. Your old man tried to renegotiate territory, thinking that might get Vitali to cool down a little."

"Renegotiate?" It's a dirty word around here. "You mean give up territory?"

"Vitali wants control of the container terminals in Bayonne and Red Hook."

The idea makes me laugh. "Fuck that. The bastard never did know when to leave well enough alone."

"Which is what your father told him in not so many words. He offered to give up the trade in Harlem instead."

"What the fuck? He wants to give up Harlem?" It's the last territory aside from Manhattan, where our family controls the drug trade. Over the years, Vitali and his crew have inched their way closer to it, waiting for their moment.

"He would if it comes to that," he states firmly. "Vitali wasn't happy about it, said he'd have an answer for him tomorrow."

I don't like it, but one thing at a time. I have to get to Emilia. Papa will be pissed that things didn't go well with Vitali, and he might decide to take it out on her. When my fingers wedge beneath the hinged handle, I pull with all my strength. It's been years since any of us have used the door, and the squeaking hinges make us both freeze, cringing.

"You better go, fast," Niccolo mutters once it looks like nobody currently patrolling the grounds heard the noise. "I'll go sit in front of your place."

"Thanks."

"Don't mention it. Just make sure your ass doesn't get caught in there." I begin to lower myself down the ladder while he closes the door, leaving me in pitch blackness until I locate the light switch.

The row of incandescent bulbs running the length of the tunnel's ceiling flicker to life. A few of the bulbs are burned out, but enough are still working to light my way. I waste no time running the tunnel's length, coming to a set of stairs carved into the house's foundation. The door at the top opens onto the pantry, which I guess is where they used to store all the crates of alcohol back in the day.

Quietly, I make my way past shelves full of dry goods

and open the door to what used to be the servants' stairs. They take me to the second floor, which seems to be quiet when I ease the door open and look down the long hall. The eastern wing is where the guestrooms are located, and I know that's where Emilia is.

Separate from the rest of the family but still on camera.

I know the layout of these rooms thanks to a lack of imagination on the part of the architect. Thankfully, there's a way to get her out without alerting anybody.

Figuring out which room is hers is no great challenge. All it takes is finding the door whose knob doesn't turn when I try it, leaving the single locked door belonging to her.

It's been a long time since I've used my lock-picking kit, but some things you don't forget. Once I've disengaged the lock, I open the door crack. "Emilia? Don't react."

Shifting on the bed tells me she knows I'm here. "Get up and make it look like you're going to the bathroom." I look up and down the hall, watching and listening. "You'll be out of range of the camera by the time you reach the door. Take your time. Don't do anything hasty."

Her feet shuffle along the floor before she pulls the door open wide enough to slip through. Her face lights up when she finds me waiting. "Luca?" she whispers before throwing herself at me.

And now that she's here, in my arms, I can breathe again. I'm home. I know everything will work out because I am holding her, and she's trembling against me, but she's holding me too, holding on tight like her life depends on it. My mouth finds hers, and I claim it, crushing her lips against mine.

She's real.

She's here.

I'm never letting her go.

"You're all right," she whispers shakily once I let her up for air, leaning back to take my face in her hands, staring at me like she's afraid it's a dream.

I know the feeling because I need to touch her face and hair, anything I can get my hands on to prove to myself she's real. "I've been so worried. I'm going crazy without you," I admit.

Nothing about what I said seems to shock her. All it does is make her rest her forehead against mine and release a shuddering sigh. "Me too. What are we going to do?" *We.* Her choice of words leaves me sighing in relief.

We're in this together.

One answer springs to mind, and I waste no time, pulling her along with me to the next room down the hall, a generic guest room that probably hasn't been used in ages. No sooner do I have the door closed, she's in my arms again so I can lift her off her feet and carry her to the bed, stumbling a little in the darkness.

"I've been worried about you," she tells me, and her arms tighten around my neck until I'm afraid I'll have to tell her to loosen up. I wouldn't, though. Not when it feels so good.

"Have they taken care of you?" I whisper as I lay her across the silk duvet.

"Yes." She clings to me, burying her face in my neck. "I even met your sister. She's a sweetheart."

"She is."

"And she told me something." I can't see her face, and I don't dare turn a lamp on in case somebody walks past and sees the light radiating from under the door. That doesn't keep me from sensing the concern I'd find etched across her features. "She told me what you did. What you promised so long as your family cared for me."

"I didn't think she knew." I wish she hadn't said

anything. That was for me to explain. Her naturally inquisitive nature, paired with the fact that she's now eighteen and thinks she's grown, have turned her into a handful.

"She knows a lot of things," she whispers with laughter at the edge of her voice. She then wraps her arms around my shoulders and pulls me close, molding herself against me. "Why did you do that? You shouldn't have done that for me."

What a question. I stroke her hair and back, letting myself soak in the pleasure of being close while I try to find the words. I already wasted too much time pretending not to care. She deserves the truth now, no matter how I struggle with it. "Don't you know by now I would do anything for you?" I murmur, my lips brushing against the top of her head. "I would even torture myself by staying away so long as I knew you were safe. There's nothing I wouldn't do for you. I've lied for you. I've disappointed my family and made things worse with our enemies. I've killed to keep you safe."

Tipping her head back, I kiss her forehead. "I would do it all again, too, because nothing in the world matters half as much as you."

"This is crazy," she whispers with a shaky laugh.

"What is?"

"I would end up having a mobster fall for me, wouldn't I?" Her fingers trail down my cheek in a gentle caress. "And I would go and fall for him."

In the darkness, I hear the emotion in her hitching breaths, feel it in the way her chin trembles when I take hold of it so our mouths can meet in a kiss that starts off slow tentative, and all-consuming.

Not for long. Heat flares to life all at once, and I give myself over to it. Something inside me cries out in joy when her body melts against mine when she runs her hands over me the way I do to her. Knowing she wants this as much as I do is a rush like nothing I've ever known. I bite her bottom lip between our tongues colliding, and a sweet moan escapes her lips.

A sudden flash of light spills over the bed and startles us both into sitting up partway, squinting at the dark figure in the doorway. "Sorry to interrupt."

Dante. I can only make out his silhouette, but I would know that snide voice anywhere.

He throws clothes onto the floor. "Get dressed," he mutters, and I assume he means Emilia. "Meet us downstairs. My father's study. Luca, you can show her the way." He slams the door, plunging us into darkness once again.

"Oh, God, Luca." All at once, she starts shaking hard enough to make the mattress vibrate. "My God, what are they going to do? What are we going to do?"

A darkness falls over me, settling into the very depths of my depraved soul, a gnawing in my gut driving me forward.

She is mine.

Nobody will harm her.

Not even my blood.

"Whatever it is, we'll get through it," I vow, and I mean it with everything I am.

21

EMILIA

Every crime scene photo I've ever studied flashes in front of my mind's eye as Luca and I walk hand in hand down the wide marble staircase leading to the main floor of the family mansion. This could very well be the only time I have a chance to see something this magnificent. That's the only word to describe it.

I wish I could appreciate the exquisite architecture, the towering ceilings, the breathtaking plasterwork, and the dramatic floor-to-ceiling windows. But all I can imagine is my blood spread across the wood-paneled walls and parquet floors of Rocco Santoro's study once we step foot inside.

He sits behind a desk that's about as long as a four-door sedan, settled back in a leather chair. Men I vaguely recognize stand to either side of the chair. The one on his right is Dante, Luca's older brother. They share the same dark good looks, though Dante's features are a bit sharper compared to Luca's sensuous mouth and sultry eyes. Dante's dark eyes practically burn with hatred as he glares across the room toward us.

The man to Rocco's left looks like one of his nephews and soldiers. Francesco, I believe his name is. His black hair is thick and wild, growing past his ears and almost brushing his shoulders. From what I remember through my research, he's a cold-blooded killer. His thin, chiseled face is as still as stone, giving away nothing. *Is he supposed to be my assassin?*

"Oh, Niccolo. Please join us." Rocco shoots a dirty look at the man who enters the room after we have, who winces at Luca as he walks past us. The elder Santoro clicks his tongue. "You know, it amazes me you boys think anything goes on in this house without my knowing about it. Like I don't have an alarm set on the tunnel doors." I don't know what that means, but Luca mutters a curse.

Niccolo is a cousin like Francesco, and he's just as violent. Although, right now, he looks more sheepish than anything else.

One of the men guarding the room from outside closes the door, leaving me alone with the lions in their den. No, not alone. Luca is still by my side, and he holds my hand tighter than ever.

"Nice to see you up and about." Rocco's lips twitch, though there's no humor behind his words. "You've caused me no small amount of trouble, young lady."

"Our entire family," Dante growls out.

"Was I speaking, or were you?" Rocco stares up at his son, almost daring him to talk back. All it does is make Dante look at the floor and clear his throat before Rocco adds, "Obviously, I'm talking about the family. Everything I do is for this family."

"I already know what Vitali said," Luca announces. "What I want to know is, what are you going to give him?"

Rocco scowls and grunts before shooting daggers at Niccolo, who's suddenly interested in the floor between his feet. "As if I would speak of such matters with her in the room." He gives Luca a mournful look. "Have I taught you nothing?"

"Can I ask a question?" Shock hits as the question leaves my mouth, and I can't believe I whispered that. My mouth got ahead of my brain. Now everybody but Luca looks at me, wearing a sneer of disgust at my audacity.

Rocco's brows lift. "You think you deserve to have your questions answered? You're a cop. You're the enemy."

"Papa…" Luca murmurs.

"Say what you want," Rocco decides, ignoring Luca.

"I'm only curious," I blow out, pushing aside the nerves that ricochet in my stomach. Have I imagined a scenario like this a hundred times? Sure, but usually, I was the one asking the questions, and they were the ones handcuffed to a table in an interrogation room. "Do they know who I am? I know you do. But do they?" It's obvious nobody wants to answer me, making me bite my tongue to hold back a frustrated scream.

Cesco purses his lips while Niccolo lifts an eyebrow in Rocco's direction. Dante only scowls at me. "We're still unsure," Rocco finally admits. "Regardless, it's a matter of principle now. They believe you are a spy for our family against their own."

"You couldn't have chosen a worse night to visit my brother's club," Dante informs me, cold with so much hate. I wouldn't care the way I do if I didn't feel like my life depended on the outcome of this meeting. Which, of course, it does, and the knowledge makes cold sweat bead at the back of my neck while I fight for every shaky breath. *I could die tonight.*

"Luca here was conducting business that had to do with the Vitali family," Rocco explains. "Which you witnessed. This started with them wanting to get their hands on you to find out what you learned… about what may or may not have been confessed to my son. The more difficult it was for them to find you, the more determined they were to get their hands on you. And now, here we are."

He shrugs like he is nothing more than a cog in the wheel with no control over anything. A leaf swept along in the wind. And it is complete bullshit. But I am also in no state to speak up for myself, standing here in what is probably Guilia's hoodie and leggings.

I've never felt less like myself, less in control.

"Can't you see what an asset she is?" Luca looks around the room, searching for backup. "She could be our inside connection. She could tell us what the cops know, keep them from getting too close. But more importantly," he adds, raising his voice a little. "She can keep tabs on the Vitali. She's worth her weight in gold. Don't you see it?" I nod, even though the idea doesn't thrill me. It doesn't have to. Luca is fighting for me, and it's an idea that only needs to keep me alive.

"We already have someone on the inside, remember?" Rocco counters without missing a beat. A man in his position is used to thinking five steps ahead at all times. It makes me sick to think we were trying to take them down when they're busy paying someone off to stay one step ahead of us.

"We could use all the help we can get," Luca stubbornly insists. "Especially when we're practically in a war. Why would we want to rid ourselves of our assets? And Papa, you know this means more to me. Does that matter?"

"Here we go again." Dante sighs, shaking his head.

If the tension and hostile looks are anything to go by, I wouldn't be surprised if he and Luca got into regular fistfights. I, for one, wouldn't mind taking a swing at him myself.

"Shouldn't you be off somewhere by now, getting fucked?" Luca snarls. "Unlike you, I have blood pumping through my veins. I'm a living, breathing person, and I didn't bust my ass keeping her alive to hand her over now to be executed."

"That was never your call, son," Rocco points out, managing to sound slightly sad about it.

Luca's growl raises the hair on the back of my neck. "She was in the wrong place at the wrong time. End of story. I have told her nothing. She saw nothing she could make a case out of. Don't you think she would've started shit for us if she could have? There is no evidence."

"She's still a detective. She has spent days with you, with us. I'm sorry, but we could never trust her." Rocco won't look at me now, saving his focus for Luca.

Is that because I don't matter? Or because he's trying like hell to convince his son this is the right thing to do?

"Besides," Rocco adds, looking over the room. "We already have a plan in place. A story for what happened to her. Everything's been worked out. There's nothing else we can do."

Shock wraps itself around my stomach and squeezes hard enough that I gag on the cold, hard fact that these men created a plan to kill me and cover it up. Men with the balls to stare blankly at me now like this is another day in the office.

"This is bullshit." Luca drops my hand, flying to his father's desk and slamming his hands on the surface. "She can't hurt us! You don't have to do this."

He whirls around, snarling when the door behind us begins to open. "Boss?" the guard asks. "Sorry, somebody out here said you're expecting him?"

"Sure, have them come in." Rocco stands, buttoning his charcoal suit jacket. "He's right on schedule. We're going to go over the finer points of the plan."

I turn my head more out of reflex than anything else. When somebody comes into a room, you look at them. Even when it's becoming increasingly clear you're in the final moments of your life, your body does things the way it would if everything were normal.

However, there is absolutely nothing normal about the presence of the man who enters Rocco's study and offers a sad grin when our eyes meet.

This is Rocco's inside man?

"Craig?" I whisper in horror before the world tilts, and my knees give out.

22

LUCA

As soon as she begins to fall, I lunge, catching her and holding her close, almost cradling her against me. They want to kill her.

She isn't worried about that now. "My partner," she whispers, staring at the tall, sandy-haired guy like she's seen a ghost. "He's my partner."

"Sorry, kid." He manages to sound sorrowful as he slides his hands into his coat pockets. "I tried to tell you to stay away from the club, didn't I? You should've listened."

Her mouth moves soundlessly for a few seconds before her eyes narrow to slits, and a guttural cry tears its way out of her chest. "You bastard! You fucking prick! All this fucking time, you were working for them? Pretending we were going to build a case?"

"Having kids isn't cheap." That's as much as he'll say, and there's nothing but frank honesty behind his statement. He's not trying to defend himself. He's stating the facts as he sees them.

My father clears his throat. "Enough. Let's get back to

business." His booming voice silences everyone into
obedience.

I help Emilia back to her feet and make sure she's
steady, though I can't imagine how she's managing it. She
has strength beyond what she revealed back at the cabin.
The woman is made of steel. "Let's talk next steps," Papa
continues. "Craig here saw to it that Luca's car was towed
from the safe house. He was careful to wipe the place for
any prints."

"I lifted prints from the bodies and placed them around
the cabin," Craig explains. "A few here and there, as if
they wore gloves most of the time. Enough to establish
their presence."

Papa folds his hands on the desk. "So, this is the story.
Vitali had Detective Washington kidnapped and taken to
the house. There's no legal record of it belonging to our
family. The crew kept her there until Craig tracked her
location and, during a shootout, killed her captors and
rescued her."

He lifts his shoulders in a parody of a shrug.
"Unfortunately, Emilia was killed in the crossfire when she
attempted to flee. She bled all over the place in front of the
cabin."

"The doctor treated my wound," she blurts out, hoping
it makes a difference. Her voice trembles, but she wears a
mask of determination to be brave to the very end. It's like
she's pulled the loose thread that will make the entire plan
fall to pieces. My heart squeezes at her courage as an
unyielding anger grips my throat.

Papa might as well yawn. He's that unbothered by her
comment, choosing to glare at Dante instead.

"We can work around that," Dante insists.

Rage leaves me shaking and biting my tongue. Dante
would love nothing more than for me to fall apart and

drive the final nail into Emilia's coffin. But I won't let that happen. Once I can trust myself, I mutter, "You have everything figured out." I look around again, seeking sympathy. It's clear Niccolo is on my side, and even Francesco looks as if he wishes he wasn't here. One of them might speak up for Emilia, but that would be too much to ask. "What about me? What about what she means to me?" I argue, grasping at what I can.

A brief flash of something like concern washes across Papa's lined face, but it blows away quickly. "We'll work that out too. Time heals everything."

I watch in shock as he gestures for Cesco to take her. This can't be happening. My own family would not betray me this way. My father would not ignore what I need. "Don't you fucking touch her," I warn, snarling at my cousin once he begins his approach.

"What do you think you're doing?" Papa asks in a menacing tone.

I launch in front of her, shaking my head at my cousin. "You're not taking her. Nobody is. Get the fuck away."

"Look at yourself," Dante counters, waving an arm toward us. "Look at what she's already done to you. She's a fucking liability, and you know it. Even if she wasn't a cop, which she is, she has fucked with your head."

Panic has begun bubbling in my gut, and now it's flooding my chest. Soon, it will fill my throat until I can't speak, so the words pour out of me in a rush. "She didn't know the fallout of what she saw at the club. I drew her into our family, and she shouldn't have to die for that. That shits on me, and I'm not going to let you kill her." I look at my father, who is silently absorbing this. "Papa. If you want her, you'll have to go through me first because I fucking love her." Her soft gasp rings out in my ears and makes me wish I had told her first.

Alone, in private, as she deserves.

Yet another regret.

Dante clicks his tongue, but our father doesn't. He blinks once, twice, blank-faced. "I know that, son."

His words land like lead. "You know, and you would still do this?"

"She is going to hurt our family, and that includes you. Being the head of a family like ours isn't all about giving everyone what they want. Sometimes, tough decisions have to be made. There are sacrifices."

Not this time. I have to make him see. "You would sacrifice what I want more than anything in the world?"

"I would if what you want most in the world wears a badge."

Emilia's voice rings out loud and clear behind me. "I resign."

It takes a hell of a lot to surprise my father, not to mention the other Santoros in the room. Even Dante reacts in shock, his brows lifting until they practically touch his hairline. "You're not serious," he accuses.

"If that's what it takes?" She looks around, almost daring everyone to meet her gaze. This is not the cowering, tear-stained girl they were expecting. "Dead serious. I quit. I'm not a cop. I'm not a detective. I'm nobody."

Dante tips his head to the side, smirking. "You're only saying that to save your neck."

"So what if I am?" Even now, with everything that's ever mattered on the line, I still get a charge out of watching Dante's mouth snap shut. "It's more than that. I found out something. Actually, two things."

"This, I'd like to hear," Papa murmurs the way he does when he's indulging Guilia. "Go ahead."

She rolls her shoulders back, and it's a gesture I'm beginning to love. "First, I don't want any part of an organization like the one Craig here is a part of. I don't know what I expected the job would be like, but it's pretty clear to me now that the concept of justice is bullshit when the bad guys have enough money to fix everything in their favor. I was young and naïve to think I could make a difference. Besides," she adds with a bitter chuckle. "If it's true that I have nerve damage, I am not interested in being a desk jockey for the rest of my career. I would rather greet shoppers at Walmart than sit behind a desk."

"A very mature perspective," Papa decides, nodding slowly. "Very intelligent. I don't much appreciate the way you referred to my family, but I can respect your point of view. What was the other point you wanted to make?"

The touch of her hand on my shoulder is soft, like a warm breeze. "If I have to resign to be with Luca, I will because I didn't know until today that I love him. And if I have to choose between him and my job, there's no decision to be made. It seems pretty obvious what I need to do."

She loves me.

The words send a shock wave through my body and leave me aching to hold, touch, and kiss her. I could shout with joy because, finally, there's a defined purpose to my life that goes beyond family loyalty. *Her. Us.* That's what I'm choosing, and I'm not alone.

My brother never did know when to keep his mouth shut. "You're only saying that because—"

Papa cuts Dante off with a single wave of his hand. "Enough. I hear you, but enough." His gaze is still trained on Emilia. "This isn't some last-ditch effort to save your life?"

Rather than answer, she asks, "Mr. Santoro, do you remember our first conversation upstairs?"

"I do."

"What was one of the first things I asked you? What did I care most about?"

His brow creases. "My son. Whether he was all right or not."

"And what did I ask for?"

The creases deepen, and this time, he sighs. "To see him."

She looks up at me, wearing a soft smile. "And after you made it sound like he told you everything about me, did I turn on him? Did I get bitter? Did I curse you out?"

I'm busy staring down at her, but I hear his soft, regretful sigh. Like he gets what she's driving at and doesn't like being proven wrong. "You did not."

Her head swings around until she's gazing his way. "So I was either very good at lying for somebody who just regained consciousness, or I was being sincere. You're a man who's seen everything. I'm sure you have sharp instincts."

She steps around me, standing front and center before my father in a challenge. I watch in awe at the woman in front of me going head-to-head with Rocco Santoro. "You tell me. Was I lying to save myself?"

She holds my father's gaze, and he fixes his weathered eyes on her, assessing her life in his hands.

The silence that hangs over the room once her voice fades away is profound. She has rocked me to my foundation. I'm too stunned to react. There's nothing I can do but stare at her, then at my father.

He draws a long breath before placing his palms on the desk, then swinging his head back and forth to look at everybody. "Craig, take your partner out of here. We're going to have a vote."

23

EMILIA

They're going to vote?

That's how they're going to decide my fate? By voting on it while I sit here and avoid anything resembling eye contact with someone who I never got along with but still would never have expected this from?

Was I that naïve?

Or was Craig that good at covering his tracks?

What might be the worst part is the sense of him trying to bring me around to his side of things. "It's not as bad as you think," he tells me as he and another two soldiers stand guard in front of the closed door separating us from Rocco's study.

The walls must be soundproofed since I can't hear a thing coming from there, but then again, I imagine Rocco wouldn't want his wife or daughter to hear how vicious he is.

This room is smaller, cheerful, even pretty. Fresh flowers fill crystal vases and China bowls, and the aroma of roses and orchids fills the air. Maybe this is where Mrs.

Santoro spends time. Maybe it helps her feel close to her husband to read here, listen to music, or pretend she doesn't know exactly what her husband does on the other side of the door.

I'm a hypocrite for thinking that way. I just declared my love for Luca minutes ago. I can't exactly look down on the woman.

"You can drop the high and mighty act," Craig continues. He's still wearing his long, black coat, his typical slacks, and a button-down shirt beneath it. His badge is partly visible, hanging from a lanyard around his neck. He looks like he could've come in directly from the station.

I had no idea. How could I have missed it?

"You don't have to speak to me," I tell him after offering an icy stare. "I don't need to hear it."

His derisive snort is almost comforting after hearing it so many times. "Face it. Everybody makes their choices. I chose to collect more money than a detective normally brings home, all so my wife and kids can be comfortable and secure."

"I'm so happy for you."

He lifts his chin, eyes narrowing dangerously. "Says the girl who offered to resign her job for the man she loves."

There's a shrewd gleam in his eye when I meet his gaze, and it makes me sick. He thinks he knows me. "That's different."

"How?"

"I'm not interested in explaining myself to you, now or ever." I stare at my clasped hands, bouncing my knee up and down. How strange it is to be sitting in a beautiful room such as this, wondering if it's the last beautiful thing I'll ever see before my eyes close forever.

I get up and approach a bowl of pristine, perfect white roses. They're lush and fragrant, and I lower my head to take a deep breath and inhale their sweetness. Roses always were my favorite.

Am I thinking of myself in the past tense?

Luca won't let them hurt me. He will not let them kill me. It's the last shred of hope I possess, and I cling to it with all my might.

"Tell me the truth." I look over my shoulder at Craig, who has the nerve to smirk. "Did you mean it when you said you loved him? You can tell me."

"Because you're so trustworthy?" I ask as a flicker of annoyance rushes through my blood. "Because we're supposed to be partners, and we need to be able to believe in each other? Since when does that matter?"

"Are you avoiding my question?" His smirk widens into a grin I would love nothing more than to slap off his face.

"Like I said, I'm not interested in speaking to you."

He tilts his head. "Even if I already know how to fix the story so you come out looking good?" He never did know when to stop. Why should now be any different?

"Really?" To say I'm skeptical would be an understatement.

"Sure. I discovered you out there, and you tried to help me fight those Vitali guys off, and you were injured. I managed to stop the bleeding long enough to get you some help. The family can take care of the specifics," he assures me, which makes me wonder how long he's been working with them. He seems very sure of himself and their influence. "Then you decide to resign after your ordeal. Really, it's cut and dry. Piece of cake."

"And you come out looking like a hero," I add since he conveniently left that part out.

The man has no shame. I already knew that. "I'm a hero either way," he states, as a matter of fact, and I can't look at him anymore.

I turn away and go to the window, though there isn't much I can see in the dark. There are floodlights mounted around the exterior of the house, but all they do is give me a view of the lawn and the wall, marking the edge of the property. I can only imagine living here would feel like a prison rather than a sanctuary, but that could be my present state of mind coloring my perception.

Luca has to come through. He has to. Everything else, we can figure out. Did Rocco look like he was coming around? I don't know whether he did or if it's simply my wanting to believe he did.

The door bursts open, and a hurricane that looks a lot like Luca rushes into the room. I'm in his arms before I know what's happening. "It's over. It's over," he groans with his lips brushing the top of my head.

"What is?" I can hardly take a breath, much less speak, thanks to the way his arms practically crush me.

"You're safe." I feel the rapid pounding of his heart, but that's nothing compared to the way my heart hammers. The room is spinning. All the strength leaves my body at once, and I'm glad Luca is here to hold me up. I believed in him. I didn't necessarily believe in the rest of them, though.

Closing my eyes and clinging to him, I say a silent prayer of thanks, letting the truth sink into my bones. I'm going to live. The family I wanted more than anything to destroy has granted me a future. It's absurd, but then life has proven itself rather ridiculous lately.

I open my eyes again at the sound of footsteps, and I find Rocco entering the room, followed by the other men. Dante doesn't bother concealing his scowl. *Is he going to be a problem?*

I hate to imagine it that way, but it's obvious he's against me sticking around. I don't see anything like that from the other two guys. In fact, Niccolo offers a grin when he sees Luca and me wrapped up in each other.

"This is contingent on you holding up your end of the bargain." Rocco still looks stern as he approaches. Luca loosens his grip on me but refuses to let go, and I'm not about to complain. "You resign, you follow along with whatever Craig tells you to tell anyone who starts asking questions. We'll work it out so our family doctor can put together a report on your injuries and treatment."

"It would be better if you claim shock," Craig decides, and the sound of his voice makes me sick, but then he's going to help ensure I get through the aftermath.

Is this what life has become? A constant compromise? Learning to live with certain things because there are other things I can't live without? Like the man who hasn't let go of me yet?

Maybe that's what life has always been, and I'm only now figuring it out.

"Yes, the less you say, the better." Rocco shrugs in an almost good-natured manner. "It's nothing personal. I hope you understand. I have people to protect."

I hope he doesn't expect me to be buddy-buddy anytime soon. I know who he is. I know what he's done. I also know I don't want to be without his son. I couldn't explain it if I took the rest of my life to find the words. It's a feeling. A certainty. Undeniable, unbreakable. From the beginning, he worked his way into my system like a drug I can't kick. I don't think I want to, either.

"I'll have one of my guys take you down to Luca's house so you can get yourself cleaned up and comfortable," Rocco decides before snapping his fingers. Francesco hops to it, going to the door and having a short conversation in the hall. "At some point, we'll get you to your apartment so you can pack up anything you want to bring along. From today on, you live here. We'll keep the apartment for you as a cover, but this is your home. If you want to be with my son, this is where you start. Do we understand each other?"

"We do." And do we ever. He wants to keep me under his thumb the way he keeps his children under his thumb. Maybe in time, things will ease up, but for now, I am living under scrutiny.

When Luca gives me a little squeeze of reassurance, I'm reminded of everything he was willing to sacrifice for me. How far he's willing to go to protect me. I have no doubt he would burn down the world if it meant my safety. The heat from that imaginary fire warms me to my core and lights up my heart. It puts everything in perspective.

I can deal with Rocco Santoro's watchful eye if it means we'll be together.

"You're staying here?" I ask when a guard steps up, waving me toward him, but Luca remains in place.

"We have some things to discuss." There's another squeeze before Luca offers a brief smile. "I'll meet you there. You'll be okay by yourself."

I'm starting to understand I have no choice. Might as well get used to following orders around here. "I'll make do."

"I'll walk with you," Craig offers, falling in step beside me. "We need to go over our story, make sure we have everything straight." *Terrific.* It's Luca I want to be with, who said he loves me, and who I love. We should be together, talking things over, finally taking the time to be together. One on one.

Instead, I'm stuck with my smirking ex-partner.

24

LUCA

I hate watching her walk away.

"Don't worry." I look at my father, watching me watch her, and I can't read his expression. "She's in good hands," he tells me.

"I want it on the record that I'm against this." Dante won't be satisfied until I knock his teeth out. Even now, he can't stand losing.

"You were outvoted," Papa reminds him, but there's no gloating involved. No chiding. It's the simple truth. "There's not much else to say."

"I meant what I said in there." My sullen brother meets my gaze. I've borne the weight of his disapproval before. This is nothing new. "She fucks up, you come to me. I take full responsibility for this."

My promise earns me nothing but a snicker. "You must have a lot of faith in her," he observes.

"I do. Get to know her. Do you understand?"

His head snaps back before he barks out a laugh loud enough to make us all wince. "Pardon me if I don't give a shit about understanding her." He snarls. "I can't even understand you. I'm not about to waste more time."

I meet his anger with blank acceptance. At the end of the day, nothing is more important than keeping Emilia safe and with me. I can let his bullshit roll off my back. "Fair enough." I got what I need. I realized a long time ago I have no need for my brother's approval.

"Leave us alone now," Papa tells him and the others. "I would like a minute alone with Luca to catch him up on the state of affairs."

The look he gives Dante could melt solid rock. It would appear my brother knows when he's fighting a lost cause since he follows our cousins out into the hall without any more arguments.

Papa shakes his head with a mournful sigh. "I don't like to see the two of you like this."

"We've always been like this," I remind him. "We're oil and water."

He isn't comforted. If anything, his frown deepens into true sorrow that radiates from him when he looks my way. "That's not going to fly once my time comes, and the family is left in his hands and yours."

Everything in me recoils from the idea. "Don't talk like that. That's not going to happen for a long time."

"I'm not so sure anymore." He walks slowly back to his study and sits at his desk. Is he playing up his age to make his argument, or has he slowed down more than I noticed before? "Right now, the way things are looking and everything hanging over our heads, it's a lot for an old man to handle. I'm not putting it on you entirely, but you're not helping things."

I perch carefully on the corner of the desk, glad we're alone together so we can speak frankly. "What made you vote in favor of letting Emilia live if it means escalating our issues with Vitali?" I question, wanting to understand.

He's never been somebody who likes explaining his choices, and it seems like this is no exception. After shifting uncomfortably in his chair, he replies, "For one thing, I'd be fooling myself to think she's the end of it. I wasn't born yesterday. Vitali isn't going to turn over a new leaf and decide he wants peace and harmony all because I had a detective murdered at his order."

"I see your point." This is why he's the head of the family. That's why Dante couldn't hope to fill his shoes, at least not yet.

Papa eyes me knowingly. "And I'm not going to have you resenting me for the rest of your life for taking her away. It would be one thing if family business involved carpentry or plumbing or some shit. I don't need my son turning against me down the line."

The idea startles me. "I would never do that," I insist.

The corners of his mouth tug upward. "You already have. I won't insult you by pretending I don't understand why you did it, but you did. And that is not something I'm going to forget."

He means it. No doubt. There's nothing to do but accept it. "I meant what I said. I'll do anything to make up for it. Whatever it is, you've got it. So long as she's safe."

"Yes, yes." He sounds tired, and I know this marks the end of that topic. "Vitali wants two of our container terminals to run their weapons and stolen merchandise through."

I wince at the idea. We've controlled those terminals for decades and collected hefty fees from outsiders in exchange for our protection of their less-than-legal shipments. "Nic told me earlier."

"So he told you I offered him the drug trade in Harlem

instead." I nod, and he continues, "I hate to lose the territory, but they've been trying to get a foot in the door up there for years.

It could stave off any immediate violence until we get everything settled and looking legit with your girl. I told him we could let bygones be bygones, that the blood that's already been shed can be forgotten."

A nice thought, but I don't have much faith. "Why do I feel like that's not going to make much of a difference to Allesandro?"

"He's looking for a reason to remind everybody his old man's way of doing things is over. No diplomacy, no working together. He wants to take by force." He rubs the back of his neck, then lifts his hands into the air. "What do I know? It's a new world. Maybe that's the way of it today. I've never been somebody who shies away from doing what needs to be done, but fuck. There used to be a code we lived by." His slumped shoulders and sagging face bring his advancing age to mind again, and pain stirs in my chest at the thought of him stepping down. It would mean the end of an era.

"We'll get through this. We always do." It's the only thing I know to be true. "I'm with you. Whatever it is we need to do."

"Sure. You've proven that so far." He is not going to let me live this down anytime soon, not that I expected anything different.

The door opens without warning, and I know who's entering the study without looking by the way his posture changes. His expression softens, and his eyes go warm. You would never know we've been engaged in conversation about possibly going to war. "*Mi amore*, what is it?"

I turn to smile at my mother, who comes to me with arms outstretched. "How good it is to see you here." At first, her touch is gentle and loving when she takes hold of my face and gazes at me through hazel eyes filled with love, but that doesn't last long. She shakes my head a little, growling. "Don't you ever do that to your mother again. No running off. We all need you here."

I cover her hands with mine, laughing even as she rattles my brain. "Yes, I know. I didn't want to upset you."

"You could've fooled me." She clicks her tongue, but there's a familiar fondness in her wry grin. "There's something I wanted to share with you."

She tucks her hand in my elbow and leads me from the study to her sitting room. I look to my father for understanding, but he only shrugs.

"How is she?" Mama asks in a conspiratorial whisper once we're alone.

I close the door, separating us from the study. I can breathe a bit easier without my father's penetrating gaze reminding me of every mistake I've ever made. "Relieved. Probably still nervous."

"Oh, your papa knew it would be a cold day in hell before I would let him kill that sweet girl." She swipes her lower lip while I gape at her in surprise. "She was only doing her job. And he should know there's nothing to be done when you fall in love."

Patting the sofa after she takes a seat, she murmurs, "Come. Sit with me."

I oblige, still shaken by the thought of my quiet, dignified mother stepping up to tell the great Rocco Santoro what to do. Her eyes shine as she leans in slightly. "You think this girl is the one?"

It's not exactly an easy topic for me to speak about openly, but if I can stand up in front of the men of my family and confess, I can do it in front of her. "Yes. I wouldn't go to all this trouble if she weren't."

Her eyes shine when tears start to well in them—tears of a happy mother. Finally, somebody around here is happy. "And does she feel the same way about you?"

Try as I might, there's no hiding a smile. "I think so. She said she loves me."

"How could she not?" She reaches out to brush my hair back from my forehead the way she's been doing since I was little.

"She would have plenty of reasons not to." I shudder to think how differently things could've gone if she hadn't opened her heart to me. How dark life would be.

"I never imagined this life for myself." She takes my hands and holds them tight. "I wasn't raised in this world. When I met your father, I knew he was where I needed to be. You don't always have to love everything a person does. It doesn't mean you don't love them. And if there's one thing I know for sure, it's that as hard as he trained you boys to be, I trained you to have good hearts. You'll need both. Especially when it comes time to start a family of your own."

A family of my own? Until the night I first set eyes on Emilia, I was sure that time wouldn't come. That the sort of love my parents have basked in for decades is a fluke. Something from the old days that no longer exists.

I'm starting to think I was wrong.

"Here. I want you to have this." She reaches into the pocket of one of her trademark cardigans and withdraws a small, black box. "I went into the safe to get it the day you brought Emilia to us. I knew right away this was the girl."

"How did you know that?" I ask with a disbelieving laugh. "She wasn't conscious."

"I didn't have to meet her. I only had to look at you and listen to you and see how it tore you apart to know she was suffering."

She opens the box, and I gasp at the sight of an antique diamond ring. I'm overwhelmed, speechless, and I can only stare in wonder for a long time before whispering, "Mama, this is beautiful."

"It belonged to my Nonna Concetta. When the time is right, you can give it to her." Love rings out in her voice as she closes the box and places it in my hand, closing my fingers around it. "I would like it to stay in the family."

My head is spinning. This is what I want. There's no doubt. It's still a lot to process, and it's clear she understands when she chuckles and pats my cheek. "Go on, be with her. She needs you."

"Thank you, Mama." I kiss her cheek, and she smiles, teary-eyed again, before I follow her orders.

She's right. Emilia needs me now.

Though she will never need me as deeply or as desperately as I need her.

25

EMILIA

What is taking him so long?

Craig is long gone, thank God. I have an appointment to meet him at the station tomorrow so we can go through an interview with Internal Affairs, in which he'll give most of the answers while I claim shock. He swears this is going to work.

All I can do is trust him.

The thought hardly soothes me.

Luca is the only thing that will comfort me now. None of this will be real until I'm in his arms again.

I've had time to take an awkward shower in his surprisingly large, well-appointed bathroom, careful to keep my bandages as dry as I can. There was no avoiding the need for it.

I'm still as tense as ever by the time I am out and toweling my hair, wrapped in a thick bathrobe I found hanging on the back of the bathroom door.

While exploring the comfortable, masculine bedroom, the front door flies open, then slams shut. The sound sends my heart into my throat. I'm still unable to trust I'm completely safe here. It might take a long time before I can consider it.

"There you are." Luca rushes into the room and gathers me in his arms before I can react, filling my world with the sound of his voice and the warmth of his body as he crushes me against him. "I couldn't stand another minute without being with you," he whispers between hard kisses against my cheeks, forehead, and chin.

"It's really over?" I ask while he unties my belt and opens the robe to run his hands over my body, making my nerves sizzle. I let the plush fabric fall to the floor and flush at the sheer lust that washes over his face.

"Yes," he grunts out, still staring lustfully before pulling his sweatshirt over his head. "And if I can't be inside you here and now, everything we went through back there will be for nothing."

"What do you mean?" I ask while heat flares to life in my core at the sight of him once he's stripped down to his tanned, chiseled body. He lowers me to the king-size bed, and I hold my arms out to him. My heart sings once he's stretched out on top of me, skin to skin, his weight pressing me against the mattress.

"I mean, I'll die otherwise," he explains with a loving grin before kissing me deeply, covering my mouth and claiming it for himself. I won't bother fighting for control. I'm his. I have been since the night we met.

"I intend to memorize every inch of your skin." His hands mold my breasts, pushing them together so he can run his tongue from one nipple to the other and back again until I have no choice but to moan his name.

"That's a good start," I whisper before moaning again when he closes his lips around my nipple and draws it into his mouth, flicking with his tongue. My helpless whimpers make him chuckle, sending delicious vibrations running through me. "Oh, yes, more of that."

"Beg me for it." He rolls his hips, and we both groan at the sizzling friction when his rigid dick rubs my mound and promises the pleasure of being filled and claimed.

I can barely catch my breath. "More," I rasp out as I grind my hips, greedy for every bit of contact I can manage. I'm so damn hungry for him. "Please, give me more. Suck my nipples… just like that."

"Oh, fuck yes." He's as helpless as I am, lost to the connection between us. This powerful, sometimes brutal man has no choice but to give himself over to me.

All it does is make me want to give more of myself to him.

And I do, arching my back to offer my body while running my hands through his hair. "Just like that," I beg before exploring the flexing, bunching muscles of his shoulders and back.

He is perfect.

He is mine.

He releases my nipple with a soft pop, moving lower, lapping at my skin as he travels to the place where the indescribable, aching heat is the most intense. "You smell so sweet," he grunts out before rubbing his nose and mouth over my pussy like some dark beast, feral and greedy for me.

Fireworks burst in my skull once his tongue makes contact with the bundle of nerves at the center of this unbearable tension. My fingers sink into his hair, and I hold his head in place, jerking my hips wildly as the fire lapping at my very soul consumes more and more of me with every lap he takes. "Luca!" I sob out, going still all at once before the tension breaks, and I sob again, shaking in the wake of sheer bliss.

"So sweet." He continues running his tongue over my lips, licking up every last drop of the juices still flowing from me. "I could drown here between your thighs, eating your pussy until you scream."

"Don't drown just yet," I whisper, pulling him back up by his shoulders, moaning when he slides his tongue into my mouth so I can taste myself. He's dripping by the time I reach between us and wrap my fingers around his thick shaft, stroking him in time with the stroking of our tongues. His deep, helpless moan sends a thrill racing through me.

I do this to him.

I have this power.

Power that burns in his eyes when he pulls back to look down at me. His hips move, and I watch as pleasure washes over his face with every stroke into my fist. "I need to be inside you," he growls out, and the sound of it makes my heart skip a beat.

"Beg me," I whisper, grinning at the brief confusion in his eyes, which soon gives way to something more feral.

Gritting his teeth, he grunts out, "I'm going to fuck you hard, Emilia. Your sweet pussy will take what I have to give you."

Oh, Jesus Christ.

He pulls his hips back before driving forward again, filling my fist, rubbing his swollen head against my mound. Wrapping a leg around his hip, I guide him to my waiting entrance, and he pushes forward, filling me all at once. "Fuck!" he gasps out, throwing his head back, while all I can do is pull him deeper with my legs. I need all of him, now, always.

He's still buried in me when his eyes open and meet mine. "You're so tight. So good." He lowers his head to kiss me before withdrawing, then surging forward again.

My God. How did I live without this?

Everything is right. Perfect. The feel of him moving inside me, taking me slowly, locking us together, and pausing before pulling back. His mouth moves over my jaw, down my throat, and the grunts he releases with every stroke only deepens my pleasure. It's sweet torture that pushes me a little closer to the finish line with every stroke. But I'm not in any hurry. I hope it never ends.

He sucks in a hiss through clenched teeth when my nails bite into his thick, firm shoulders. I didn't know I was gripping him that way. Part of me is still afraid I'll lose this. That I'll lose him. That it's not real. That the happiest moment of my life is nothing but a dream.

"Tell me this is real," I beg, holding him close while the tension builds. "Please. Tell me."

He surprises me by slamming home, sending shock waves rolling through me. "Does that feel real?" he whispers, watching me react before he does it again. And again.

"Y-yes!" I gasp, then moan when he grinds against my clit. I'm going to lose my mind if this goes on much longer. I can't take it. It's too much, too good, too hot, too everything.

"This is real." He loses his rhythm as his pace picks up. Now he's pounding me, gritting his teeth, taking me hard, and making tears of joy spring to my eyes when he repeats one word. "Mine. Mine. Mine."

His. I'll never get tired of hearing it. "Yes!" I cry out, meeting his strokes, reveling in the sight of him losing himself as I do the same. By the time he slams home with an earsplitting roar, I'm coming apart around him.

After floating in blissful darkness, the sound of his ragged breaths brings me back to the present. He's sprawled out on top of me, his face against my neck.

My Luca.

I don't have the first idea how it happened. I only know I'm glad it did. My heart floods with unimaginable tenderness before I whisper, "I love you."

"You'd better." He raises his head, wearing a smirk. "I don't know what else I could do to prove how much I love you."

"You don't need to prove it," I assure him while running my leg over his. "Though if you're feeling ambitious, we can stay here in bed, and you can keep doing that to me all night long."

A devilish light glows in his eyes. "As if I wasn't planning on it," he growls out before devouring my throat while I giggle helplessly.

———

"This is weird." My palm is sweaty, but I'm not about to let go of Luca's hand as we cross the lawn on our way up to the main house. "I can't help thinking somebody's going to jump out and kill me."

"They won't. You have nothing to worry about." He smiles at me before raising our clasped hands so he can kiss mine, then murmurs, "This is the first day of the rest of our lives together."

I love the idea. It warms my heart and makes an already sunny day seem brighter, even if my pulse still flutters with nerves as we enter the mansion.

If he believes we're safe, I have to believe it too. Right? Putting my trust in anyone but myself isn't ideal at this point and is something that won't happen overnight. But I'll keep that to myself.

Right away, a curly-headed tornado sweeps across the

grand entry hall and throws her arms around me. "We'll be sisters, I just know it," Guilia gushes.

"Take it easy, kiddo." Luca laughs, and it's clear when he beams at her equally enthusiastic hug that he adores her. "Let's not scare her off, okay?"

Right away, she backs off, chewing her lip before nodding. "It's a sausage fest around here," she groans out. "I can't afford to lose an ally."

Our laughter echoes off the marble and wood in the expansive space and deep down, I can't help but hope that maybe, just maybe, this could be the start of a new friendship.

We push farther into the hall as the three of us walk to the dining room for breakfast.

Luca explained the daily ritual during one of the breaks we took overnight.

We never did sleep.

There was too much to talk about between the breathtaking orgasms.

With the family taking time to be together during such tense circumstances, the dining room is full of voices once we reach it. It's a little overwhelming at first—they're all so loud. Rocco and his wife, Isabella, are seated at opposite ends of a long table. Niccolo and Francesco are in the middle of telling a story that makes the woman of the house laugh softly and swat at them with her napkin. Dante sits at his father's right, and the two of them are engaged in a serious conversation.

I shudder to think what they're talking about, but it's probably murder, money laundering, and all sorts of illegal activities at the top of their list. As I glance over at the father-son duo, I can't help but notice the intense aura that surrounds them like a dark cloud hanging over their heads, a reminder of the secrets and power that come with their mafia connections. Their hushed conversation is a window into a world I never thought I'd be a part of, and it sends a chill down my spine.

A handful of guards are scattered around, eating where they stand, taking food from a credenza loaded with covered chafing dishes.

The aroma filling the room makes my mouth water.

"Look who I found!" Guilia sings out before practically skipping over to her father's chair and kissing his cheek. "Good morning, Papa."

His expression softens when he gazes up at his daughter. "Good morning, Guilia."

Right away, she asks, "Can I take Emilia shopping for new clothes? She can't keep wearing mine. She deserves her own things."

"Could you ever wait your turn?" Dante asks, and for once, he doesn't seem angry or sullen. He is more like an exasperated older brother who loves his sister.

She blows out a dismissive snort. "Like you ever stop pestering Papa. I'd be twenty-five by the time I got a chance to speak to him."

I can't believe it, but I almost wish I could feel I was a part of this. A family I've detested for everything they symbolize, yet right now, they seem painfully normal. That is until Dante's gaze hardens upon meeting mine.

It's going to take a very long time for him to come around. Rocco, at least, offers a curt nod before turning back to his oldest child, but Dante holds up a hand to take a call coming through on his cell.

Isabella, Luca's mother, waves us over with enthusiasm, and I realize we've never officially met. I can see where Guilia gets her dark beauty from. We're on our way across the room with Luca leading the way when Dante releases a sharp grunt that plunges the room into silence.

"We're sure? It's confirmed?" The sound of his voice sends a chill down my spine, and I look at Luca, but he's focused on his brother. Guilia's wide-eyed stare is full of fear, while Isabella sits ramrod straight in her high-backed chair, her face still, masking the terror inside her bones.

Dante rises, ending the call, dropping the phone on the table. "Our terminals," he grits out through clenched teeth as his face turns red. "Red Hook. Bayonne. Somebody planted explosives. A bunch of guys working down there were killed, and equipment was destroyed."

Luca's hand grips mine tighter than before, and his knuckles press into my skin. "Vitali was supposed to give his answer today, wasn't he?" he asks his father in an ominously quiet voice. "On whether he'd accept your offer."

Rocco nods slowly, locking eyes with his wife for a moment before sighing sorrowfully. "He's just given us his answer. He wants to go to war."

Isabella's eyes shut tight, her face contorted with pain.

Luca's eyes hit mine. It feels like a storm of emotions, a turbulent sea of sadness, anger, and fear that wraps its way around my heart.

I don't have to ask what it means. I already know.

Luca and I only just found each other.

Now, a war might blow us apart.

To be continued....

WANT MORE?

Want to see what happens next with Luca and Emilia?

Stolen Love is Book 2 in The Elite Mafia of New York out March 16th.

It's Forbidden.
Completely Wrong.
But oh so damn right.

Preorder now from Missy's Website.
https://authormissywalker.com/collections/elite-mafia-of-new-york-series

ALSO BY MISSY WALKER

ELITE MAFIA OF NEW YORK SERIES
Cruel Lust*

Stolen Love

Finding Love

SLATER SIBLINGS SERIES
Hungry Heart

Chained Heart

Iron Heart

ELITE MEN OF MANHATTAN SERIES
Forbidden Lust*

Forbidden Love*

Lost Love

Missing Love

Guarded Love

SMALL TOWN DESIRES SERIES
Trusting the Rockstar

Trusting the Ex

Trusting the Player

*Forbidden Lust/Love are a duet and to be read in order.

*Cruel Lust is a trilogy and to be read in order

All other books are stand alones.

JOIN MISSY'S CLUB

Hear about exclusive book releases, teasers, discounts and book bundles before anyone else.

Sign up to Missy's newsletter here:
www.authormissywalker.com

Become part of Missy's Private Facebook Group where we chat all things books, releases and of course fun giveaways!

https://www.facebook.com/groups/
missywalkersbookbabes

ACKNOWLEDGMENTS

To my three editors; Chantell, Kay and Nicki I couldn't do this without you.

The same can be said for my Beta team. Maria, Ella, Saskia and Lauren.

To my amazing family, I want to express my heartfelt gratitude for your enduring patience and support. You've been there for me through the ups and downs, and I love you so very much.

To all my wonderful fans, it's truly a surreal experience for me. You've taken these characters that have been living rent-free in my head and embraced them with open arms. It's like watching a dream come to life. Writing their stories is one thing, but having you read them and rooting for them, well, that's something else entirely. Your support means the world to me, and I can't thank you enough for being on this incredible journey with me. Here's to many more adventures together!

I can't wait for you to see what's next as I continue to write steamy romances with Happy Ever Afters.

Missy x

ABOUT THE AUTHOR

Missy is an Australian author who writes kissing books with equal parts angst and steam. Stories about billionaires, forbidden romance, and second chances roll around in her mind probably more than they ought to.

When she's not writing, she's taking care of her two daughters and doting husband and conjuring up her next saucy plot.

Inspired by the acreage she lives on, Missy regularly distracts herself by visiting her orchard, baking naughty but delicious foods, and socialising with her girl squad.

Then there's her overweight cat—Charlie, chickens, and border collie dog—Benji if she needed another excuse to pass the time.

If you like Missy Walker's books, consider leaving a review and following her here:

instagram.com/missywalkerauthor
facebook.com/AuthorMissyWalker
tiktok.com/@authormissywalker
bookbub.com/profile/missy-walker